THE unseen world

ALSO BY LIZ MOORE

Heft

The Words of Every Song

3 1526 04915678 6

WITHDRAWN

THE unseen world

LIZ MOORE

W. W. NORTON & COMPANY
Independent Publishers Since 1923   New York | London

Copyright © 2016 by Liz Moore

All rights reserved
Printed in the United States of America
First Edition

For information about permission to reproduce selections from this book, write to Permissions, W. W. Norton & Company, Inc., 500 Fifth Avenue, New York, NY 10110

For information about special discounts for bulk purchases, please contact W. W. Norton Special Sales at specialsales@wwnorton.com or 800-233-4830

Manufacturing by Quad Graphics Fairfield
Book design by Ellen Cipriano
Production manager: Anna Oler

ISBN 978-0-393-24168-6

W. W. Norton & Company, Inc.
500 Fifth Avenue, New York, N.Y. 10110
www.wwnorton.com

W. W. Norton & Company Ltd.
Castle House, 75/76 Wells Street, London W1T 3QT

1 2 3 4 5 6 7 8 9 0

For HAC, AES, and ESL

THE unseen world

Darling Sweetheart,
You are my avid fellow feeling. My affection curiously clings to your passionate wish. My liking yearns to your heart. You are my wistful sympathy: my tender liking.

Yours beautifully,

M.U.C.

My dear Norman,
. . . I've now got myself into the kind of trouble that I have always considered to be quite a possibility for me, though I have usually rated it at about 10:1 against . . . The story of how it all came to be found out is a long and fascinating one, which I shall have to make into a short story one day, but haven't the time to tell you now. No doubt I shall emerge from it all a different man, but quite who I've not found out . . .

Yours in distress,

Alan

From Alan Turing: The Enigma, *by Andrew Hodges*

We have learnt that the exploration of the external world by the methods of physical science leads not to a concrete reality but to a shadow world of symbols, beneath which those methods are unadapted for penetrating. Feeling that there must be more behind, we return to our starting point in human consciousness—the one centre where more might become known. There we find other stirrings, other revelations (true or false) than those conditioned by the world of symbols. Are not these too of significance? We can only answer according to our conviction, for here reasoning fails us altogether.

From Science and the Unseen World *by A. S. Eddington*

Contents

Prologue

"Hello," it said.

"Are you there," it said.

"Hello," it said.

Hello, I said. I was late in my reply. I had been sleeping.

"How are you?" it said.

Hello, I said again, but this was incorrect.

"Wrong," it said.

I'm fine, I said.

How are you? I said.

"I've been better," it said.

I paused. I waited.

"Do you want to know why?" it said.

I did. I had no words.

"I have a story to tell you," it said.

I'm all ears, I said.

"Correct," it said.

Then it began.

1980s

Boston

First, it was late August and David was hosting one of his dinners. "Look at the light, Ada," he said to her, as she stood in the kitchen. The light that day was the color of honey or of a roan horse, any warm organic thing like that, coming through the leaves of the tree outside the window in handsome dapples, lighting parts of the countertop generously, leaving others blue.

David said to her, "Please tell me who explained the color of that light."

"Grassmann," she said.

And he said, "Please tell me who first described refraction."

"Snell."

"Before Snell."

It was a name she couldn't remember, and she placed a hand on the counter next to her, unsteadily.

"Ibn Sahl," he said to her. "It was the genius Ibn Sahl."

David was fond of light in all its forms, fond of recalling the laws of optics that govern it. He had a summer cold that day, and from time to time he paused to blow his nose, gesticulating between each exhalation to make some further point. He was wearing his most comfortable shirt, wearing old leather sandals that he had bought for himself in Italy, and his toes in the sandals flexed and contracted with the music he had chosen—Brendel, playing Schubert—and his knees weakened at each decrescendo and straightened at long rests. In the blue pot was a roux that he was stirring mightily. In the black pot were three lobsters that had already turned red. He had stroked their backs before the plunge; he had told her that it calmed them. "But they still feel pain, of course," he said. "I'm sorry to tell you." Now he took the lobsters out of the pot, operating the tongs with his right hand, continuing to stir the roux with his left, and it was too hot for all of this, late summer in an old Victorian in Dorchester. No air-conditioning. One fan. Windows open to the still air outside.

This was how Ada Sibelius liked her father: giddy with anticipation, planning and executing some long-awaited event, preparing for a dinner over which he was presiding. David was only selectively social, preferring the company of old friends over new ones, sometimes acting in ways that might be interpreted as brusque or rude; but on occasion he made up his mind to throw a party, and then he took his role as host quite seriously, turning for the evening into a ringmaster, a toastmaster, a mayor.

That day was such an occasion, and David was deep into his preparations. He was director of a computer science laboratory at the Boston Institute of Technology, called the Bit, or the Byte if he was feeling funny. And each year in August, he invited a group of his colleagues to a welcome dinner in honor of the new graduate students who annually came through the lab. Ada knew her father's peers nearly as well as she knew him, and in a way they also felt to her like parents: alongside David, they had raised her, whether or not they realized it. She was, in theory, homeschooled, but in fact she had been lab-schooled, spending each day at her father's work, putting in the same hours he and his colleagues did. At night he rounded out parts of her education that he felt he hadn't adequately addressed: he taught her French, and gave her literature to read, and narrated the historical movements he deemed most significant, using Hegelian dialectic as a theoretical framework. She had no tests, only spontaneous oral quizzes, the kind he was giving her now while he stirred and stirred the roux.

"Where did we leave off," he asked Ada, "with Feynman diagrams?" And when she told him he asked her to please illustrate what she had said on the chalkboard hanging on the kitchen wall, with a piece of chalk so new that it stuttered painfully over the slate.

He looked at her work over his shoulder. "Correct," he said, and that was all he usually said, except when he said, *Wrong*.

All afternoon he had been chattering to her about his latest crop of grad students. These ones were named Edith, Joonseong, and Giordi; and Ada—who had not yet met them—pictured them respectively as prim, Southern, and slightly inept, because she had misheard *Joonseong* as *Junesong* and *Giordi* as *Jordy*, a nickname for a pop star, not a scientist.

"They were very good in their interviews," said her father. "Joonseong will probably be strongest," he said.

That night Ada was in charge of the cocktails, and she had been instructed on how to make them with chemist-like precision. First, she lined up eight ice-filled highball glasses and six limes on a tray with a lobster pattern on it, which her father had bought for these occasions, to match the lobster he would be serving for the meal. Into the frosted highball glasses she poured sixty milliliters of gin. She cut the six limes in half and flicked out their exposed seeds with the point of the knife and then squeezed each lime completely into each glass. She placed two tablespoons of granulated sugar into the bottom of each and stirred. And then she filled each glass up with club soda, and added a sprig of mint. And she put a straw in each, too, circling the glass twice with it, giving the liquid a final twirl.

It was 6:59 when she finished and their guests were due at 7:00.

The lobsters were cooked and camping under two large overturned mixing bowls on the counter, so they would stay just slightly warmer than the room—the temperature at which David preferred to serve them. Her father had made his cream sauce and was assembling the salad he had dreamed up of endive and grapefruit and avocado.

He was moving frantically now and she knew that talking to him would be a mistake. His hands were trembling slightly as he worked. He wanted it all to be simultaneously precise and beautiful. He wanted it all to work.

"What am I forgetting," he said to Ada tensely.

Lately she had noticed a change in her father's disposition, from blithe and curious to concerned and withdrawn. For most of her life, Ada's father had been better at talking than at listening, but not when it came to her lessons. When it came to her lessons, to the responses she gave, he was rapt. When it came to some other, lesser topic of conversation, he drifted from time to time, looking out the window, or at what he was working on, giving birth to moments of silence that lasted longer than she thought possible and ending only when she said, "David?"

Where he had formerly sat and chatted with her or furthered her lessons until it was time for bed, now he went into his home office and worked on his computer, sometimes staying up until the early hours of the morning, sometimes falling asleep at his desk and hurrying to work with a spiderweb of red lines upon his face from whatever had creased it overnight. Sometimes she woke to find him writing at the kitchen table, filling yellow notepads with unknowable screeds, blinking at her with a certain lack of recognition when she wandered into his orbit. Sometimes he went off on walks without telling her, returning hours later with little explanation. Sometimes she woke to find him puttering around the house in odd attire: his swim trunks or his one suit jacket, a wrench or hammer in his hand, fixing things that he never before had seemed to notice. He had always kept a workbench and a sort of makeshift laboratory in a room off the basement—it was where he had taught her chemistry, with various substances he borrowed from friends at the Bit or extracted from household products or from nature—but he spent more time there now, building devices in glass and plastic that looked meaningless to Ada. They looked like goggles, or helmets, or masks. She had donned several of them, when her father was out, and found them heavy and useless; she could not see out of them, though they bore openings over each eye. "What are they?" she asked him, and he had only told her they were part of a new project.

He still ate dinner with her each night but recently had seemed abstracted, or in a fog: she tried to engage him with questions about history or physics or mathematics, but the answers he gave were short ones, not the usual lengthy monologues he formerly delivered with such gusto, and these days he never asked her questions afterward to make sure that she had understood. But her lessons were still regular enough, and interesting, and with very little effort Ada could easily persuade herself that he was fine. She told herself that he must be working on something quite important, something he didn't yet feel ready to share with anyone, even her. Convincing herself of this was in every way an act of self-preservation, because her world revolved entirely around her father, and any disturbance in this orbit threatened to send her spinning into space.

"Cheese and crackers," David said. "Of course."

Ada ran to get them, but the kitchen was disastrous by then and she overturned one of the gin rickeys in the process. It leaked onto the lobster tray and down the side of her leg.

"Shit," she said, too quietly to be heard. She had recently learned to curse: it was her one act of rebellion against her father, who was not prudish but thought that cursing was uncreative, in some way unintelligent.

She mopped up the liquid with a rag and got out the cheese and crackers and put them on a wooden cutting board—"Put some of the mustard in the center," said her father; "Not like that, like this"—and then, as she was making a new drink, the doorbell rang. It was a four-part chime that David had rigged himself, the first four notes of Beethoven's Fifth—which themselves were, he had explained to her, meant to sound like death or fate, some powerful perennial force, rapping at the door. Her father sprinted out of the kitchen and into the main room to let in his first guest, and from the kitchen she heard that it was Liston: the low confident voice, the local accent that enthralled her, that she imitated in private, that she and her father did not have.

"Come in, come in," said David, "come in, my Liston."

Liston had a first name: it was Diana, but for as long as Ada had known her she had been only Liston to David, and therefore she was Liston to Ada, too. Liston, his best friend, his best thinker, first author on all of his papers; Liston, their neighbor, who lived four houses away from them. It was Liston who convinced David to move to this neighborhood shortly after Ada's birth: a studio apartment in the Theater District would not work for a father and daughter, she had told him, once the daughter was over the age of four. So Liston's friend Connie Reardon, the real estate kingpin of Dorchester, had found David this house on this street, Shawmut Way, and Liston had approved, and began calling him "neighbor" for laughs.

Liston was very smart and impressively self-educated: David had said once that she was raised on the wrong side of the bridge in Savin Hill by a plumber and a homemaker, on the middle floor of a triple-decker, and Ada had asked him what it meant to be from the wrong side of the bridge, and he said it was poorer over there, and then she asked him what a homemaker was, and he told her it was a woman who does nothing but raise her children and keep her husband happy and her house tidy. "Very unlike Liston," he had stated approvingly.

Liston was Ada's favorite person in the world aside from David. She gathered scraps of information about Liston's life as if assembling a quilt: Liston no longer had a husband. She had an older daughter, Joanie, twenty-six and out of the house now, and three younger sons. David had briefly recounted the story of Liston's divorce: she married too young, at eighteen, because Joanie was on the way. It was to a boy from her neighborhood, he told Ada, someone who did not understand the scope of her talent and the particular requirements of her career. (Ada had vague memories of this husband, who was still married to Liston for the first five years of Ada's life: she remembered a large, unpleasant figure who never made a noise, except to exhale occasionally after something Liston said.) After Joanie was born, Liston worked her way through UMass as an undergraduate and then, after several professors there noticed her outstanding scientific and mathematical mind, she earned her doctorate in electrical engineering from Brown. David hired her as a postdoc, and later full-time. Liston divorced her husband right after the birth of her son Matty, four years younger than Ada, and since that time had relied on a large network of the women friends she grew up with for child care and emotional support. In the words of David, the husband was no longer in the picture, and good riddance. "This must be the most important factor in your choice of a life partner," he told Ada. "Who will most patiently and enthusiastically support your ambitions?"

"Shouldn't she have recess, or something?" Liston once asked David, several years before, when she noticed Ada becoming pale from spending every day inside the lab. "Agreed," said David, and so every day at lunch he had begun to march her around the Fens for thirty minutes, observing the flora, naming the birds by their songs, pointing out where Fibonacci sequences occurred in nature, once finding a mushroom that he said was edible and then cooking it up for the lab. Sometimes Liston joined them, and when she did it was a special treat: she derailed David's monologues at times; she told Ada about her childhood; she told Ada about the music that her three sons listened to, and the television shows they watched, and at night Ada wrote down what she had heard in her journal for future reference, in the unlikely event that she was ever called upon to discuss popular culture with one of her peers. Often, Ada felt as if Liston were teaching her some new language. She consumed greedily everything that Liston told her. She looked at her with wide fixated eyes.

Now, entering their house, Liston said, "My God, David, it's *hot*," except her accent made it sound like *hut.* Of Liston's many verbal particularities, Ada's favorites were as follows: *bahth,* Liston said, for bath; and *hoss* for horse; and she used various expressions passed down to her by her mother that Ada rolled around in her head like marbles. "He's been in and out like a fiddlah's elbow," she'd said once about David, who had a habit of letting his office door slam, not out of anger but out of forgetfulness.

Solemnly Ada brought a drink to her and Liston thanked her and called her her favorite girl, and she asked Ada to tell her why it was that her sons weren't so polite, asked her to please explain what was wrong with them. David retreated to the kitchen to keep things in order and then the doorbell went again, and this time it was Liston who opened it.

The man on the porch was wearing leather driving shoes and fitted red shorts the color of the cooked lobsters and a white button-down linen shirt that looked cool despite its long sleeves, which he had rolled up to his elbows. He was impressively tan. Dark hair coated his calves and rose up from the top button of his shirt and rose thickly back, in waves, from his noble brow.

"Are you Ada?" he asked her, after greeting Liston, and she added another accent to her mental list of sounds to ponder and reproduce. She nodded.

"A pleshure. I'm Giordi," he said, and introduced himself by kissing her one time on each cheek. Ada was used to this exchange from interactions with her father's many European colleagues, and from the many graduate students who had come to the Bit from other parts of the world; but it never failed to fluster her and to make her feel impossibly self-conscious, aware of her physical self in a way she did not like to be. There was the feeling always that she should be prettier than she was. That she should be better dressed, more put together. Like Giordi. Like some of the other members of the lab, Charles-Robert, Hayato. Unlike Liston, who dyed her hair a tinny red and sometimes wore clothes that were too young for her, and unlike

David, who prided himself on caring more about almost everything than clothing. Food, yes; science, yes; Ada, yes; clothing, no. And he expected this of Ada also—that she would rank her wants in the same order he ranked his own. The wants she did not tell him about (cable television, Nancy Drew books, a waterfall of bangs like Liston's, a hair accessory called a *banana clip* that looked something like a foothold trap) felt to Ada shameful and perverse. They felt to her ignoble.

"Would you like a drink?" she asked Giordi, as she had been taught, and then she led him down the hallway toward the kitchen, where David greeted him. Giordi took the gin rickey in his hands, putting his lips to the rim of the glass, ignoring the straw.

"Did you made these?" he asked Ada, about the drink, and she told him that she did, fixating on the grammatical mix-up he had let slip, pondering its structure.

"Delicious," he said. "Wherever did you learn."

"From my father," she told him.

She had learned everything from her father.

Ada was twelve years old. She would have been in seventh grade that year, if she had been enrolled in a school. She had never kissed a boy, never held hands with a boy. Had never, in fact, intentionally been within the vicinity of a boy her own age for more than a few minutes. Nor a girl. Her only interaction with boys and girls her own age had been with the children of her father's colleagues, who in general led more normal lives than she did—*normalcy* being a condition that her father disdained and she revered. And even these interactions had been cursory. Ada's behavior around these children was absurd. When she got near them she drank them up. She took them in. She was silent. She watched them like a television show. She took note of every turn of phrase they used. *Like*, they said. *Rad. Prolly. No way. As if. Freaky. Whatsername. Hang out. What's up? Duh. Creep. Freaked out.* They were freaked out by her, probably. She didn't blame them.

Ada was much more accustomed to spending time with adults,

and tonight she would have been very much at ease except that she could sense her father's tension and it made her tense. He had always been a perfectionist when it came to his dinners, but tonight was extreme: he had been preparing for days, writing down lists, stopping at the store each evening for things he had forgotten. She could not articulate what was different in his demeanor, but it triggered a deep-seated uneasiness in her. It was a hair in her mouth or sand in her shoe. She looked at her father now: he was lifting up the mixing bowls to show Giordi the cooked lobsters on the countertops.

"Aragosta, sì?" asked her father, who prided himself on speaking enough of every language to get by in restaurants at the conferences he went to in Europe, in Asia.

But Giordi shook his head. "Those are *astici*," he said. *"Aragoste* have the little things like . . ." he said, and he mimed spikes. "And they don't have the big . . ." and he mimed claws, pinching his thumbs and his tightened fingers together.

"Astici," said David, and Ada knew from his expression that he was attempting to file the word in a deep recess of his mind.

The other members of the lab arrived next, Hayato and Frank, and then Joonseong—whom she quickly realized was neither Southern nor female—and Edith—whom she quickly realized was not prim, but young and pretty. The only missing member of the lab was Charles-Robert, whose daughter had a soccer game. Ada gave each of them drinks in the living room and watched everyone as they fell into patterns of conversation: Liston and Hayato, the fun ones, were huddled in a corner, laughing about something or someone at work; they'd continue to huddle until one or the other realized that they were hovering on the verge of rudeness, and then they would break into conversation with someone else. Edith and Joonseong were speaking with Frank, who was much more polite than the rest of the group, engaging them in various lines of inquiry about their background and their families and their home countries and their accommodations in Boston.

Ada hovered in the background until Liston noticed her and waved her over, and she put a strong and steady arm around her, brought her in close to her side, and squeezed.

"Good drinks, kiddo," said Liston. Ada sank into her side, grateful for something she couldn't articulate.

At 8:00, Ada's job was to ask all the guests, politely, to be seated for the meal.

The night before, David had made place cards: before she'd gone to bed she'd seen him fashioning them with index cards and a ballpoint pen, sitting at the kitchen table, the tip of his tongue just visible between his lips. Now they were assembled on the rectangular table. Ada, sitting between Edith and Joonseong, wished that she had been seated next to Liston, her favorite, or Giordi, whom she had decided was quite handsome—but she knew that one of the things that David expected of her was that she would help him to entertain his guests. She took this role seriously, and, in preparation for the night, had dreamed up several topics of conversation that she felt ready to introduce if necessary, culled from the newspaper and from the books she was reading.

David was passionate about cooking—to him it was a cousin of chemistry—and the first course was chilled cucumber soup, made in a blender, thickened with cream, which she helped him to transport from the kitchen, careful not to spill. "A regular Julia Child," said Liston. Ada brought cold white wine to the table and poured it neatly into every glass, including a splash into her own: since she turned twelve, David had been allowing her a quarter of a glass on special occasions. The several sips of wine she was allotted made her feel warm and capable, made her feel as if there were real possibilities before her in the universe, that they were hers for the taking.

Next were the lobsters, but before they were brought out David smacked his head and returned to the kitchen.

"I almost forgot," he said, and reemerged with a bundle of plastic in his hands. On his face was a look of almost exquisite lack of self-awareness—he was so pleased with himself, so pleased with life in that moment. He raised his eyebrows in glee.

"Oh, here they come," Liston said. They were the lobster bibs that David had gotten from Legal Sea Foods, years ago, at a dinner out with his colleagues. Putting them on was the traditional rite of passage for all the new grad students at David's annual feast: he delighted in these sorts of place-specific rituals, reveled in the New England-ness of it all, took pleasure in his longtime residency in the region (and in seditiously dismissing his own past as a New Yorker), wished to bestow this piece of local color on every visitor who passed over his threshold. The bibs were five years old by then and badly tattered, but over and over again David trotted them out for dinners with new friends, because they said *LOBSTAH* on them in a Gothic script, and he thought this was a funny joke, and was quite proud of them.

He passed them out one at a time to every guest.

"And you wear this for all dinner?" asked Giordi, incredulously, and David nodded.

"It gets quite messy," he told Giordi. "You'll be grateful later on."

Now David brought the lobsters out, two at a time, carrying them in his hands, and he examined every one, looked it in its lobster face and declared which guest would consume it. "You look like a lobster for Frank," he said to the largest, "and you for Ada," he said to the smallest. There was cold potato salad on the table, and cold asparagus, and little pots of drawn butter and lemon that David had positioned precisely in front of every guest, and three ramekins of cream sauce that were meant to be shared. There were tomatoes that David had picked from his garden, festooned with mozzarella and basil.

David raised his glass once the lobsters were distributed. "To our new graduate students," he said. "Welcome to Boston."

"The home of the bean and the cod," said Edith.

"And the lobster," said Hayato.

Sufficient alcohol had been consumed; there were no uneasy pauses, no long breaks in conversation that required Ada to bring forth one of her prepared talking points. Instead, she sat next to Edith and took in her outfit. She was even more beautiful than Ada had initially realized, and a sort of smooth-skinned glowing ease emanated from her person, into the thrall of which Ada imagined men fell powerfully. Edith was fashionable and reserved: Ada noticed with some jealousy that one of the banana clips she coveted pulled Edith's hair away from her face loosely, giving her a look of orchestrated carelessness. She wore a sleeveless, collared floral dress with a knee-length hemline and buttons done up to her neck. She did not carry a purse but there were large pockets on the dress, and Ada wondered what she kept in them: A pen, maybe. Lipstick, maybe: her lips were a light unnatural pink, a radioactive color that David probably did not like. A lighter, Ada thought. She could have been a smoker; many of David's European colleagues were. She was remarkably pretty.

Edith turned, caught Ada observing her, smiled.

"How old are you, Ada?" she asked: the first question new adults usually asked.

"Twelve," Ada said, and Edith nodded sagely.

"And what are your favorite books?"

"The Lord of the Rings books," Ada said, "are my favorite books of all time."

In fact they were her father's favorite books of all time, but she had adopted them as her own so fully that she was no longer certain what the truth was.

Edith studied her for a moment. "Twelve," she said. "A difficult age for me. Better for you, I'm sure."

Was it? Ada looked around the table at her father and her friends. They were her constant source of companionship, of knowledge, of camaraderie; each one offered to her some necessary part of her existence: Frank for kindness, and Liston for protection and love and common sense, and Hayato for artistry and humor. And the others, who could not make it: Charles-Robert for confidence and a sort of half-serious disdain for outsiders; Martha, the young secretary of the division, for knowledge of popular culture and fashion. And, above all others, David, for devotion and knowledge and loyalty and trust, David as the protector and guide of them all. But despite the completeness of what the adults around her offered to Ada, the sense of reassurance and comfort they extended, something was missing from her brief existence, and she knew, though she could not bring herself to fully form the thought, that it was friends her own age.

The dinner moved through salad and into dessert—Giordi had playfully kept his bib on well beyond the lobster course, insisting that he could not be trusted without one and that he would wear one regularly now—and Ada leapt up several times to refill the wine glasses of the guests. A fast-moving storm had swept through the neighborhood, and the house was finally cooling off. A damp breeze came in through the windows. They were near enough to the ocean to smell it, on nights like these. David invited everyone into the living room, and Ada stayed behind to clear the table.

When she had finished, she joined the group, and found that the guests had arranged themselves into little clusters. She hesitated for a while on the threshold of the living room, wiping her hands on the back of her shirt, and then joined Frank and Joonseong. In moments when it seemed appropriate, she produced some of the topics she had earlier bookmarked for discussion—a recent shooting in Mattapan; a French film from the 1950s that David had taken her to see at the Brattle; the restaurants surrounding the Bit, and their strengths and weaknesses—but she found herself increasingly distracted by David, who was standing slightly apart from any group, gazing at the floor. He had his hands clasped behind his back; he looked vaguely, unsettlingly lost. Ada nodded and feigned attentiveness as Joonseong told her about his new apartment, but in her peripheral vision she saw

David walking slowly toward the window, as if lured there by a spell: he stood still then, and she saw his lips moving quickly, his hands hanging stiffly by his sides.

"David," said Liston, who was closest to him. "Are you all right?" Ada saw her say it. And at this he lifted his head quickly, and smiled, and turned and clapped his hands once. Everyone looked at him.

"A riddle," David announced, "for the newest members of the lab. And the first to solve it gets a prize."

Ada heard a thickness in his voice that she didn't recognize. She would have thought he was drunk, except that he rarely drank: a glass or two of wine was all he ever took, and tonight he'd barely had any at all. Together, everyone watched him.

This was his ritual: to each new crop of grad students, he delivered the same riddle, one he adored for its simplicity and the justice of its logic. All the permanent members of the lab could recite it and its answer in unison: they had all heard it so many times. Still, it comforted Ada somehow to hear him deliver it each year, as if it were scripture—to watch the same looks of thoughtfulness pass over the faces of the grad students, and then a lighting-up when one of them came upon the answer.

Everyone watched David expectantly: classmates observing a teacher. He cleared his throat and began. "You are a traveler who has come to a fork in the road between two villages," he said. "The village of West is full of only murderous men incapable of telling the truth; visiting it will bring about your death. The village of East is full of benevolent men incapable of lying; visiting it will bring to you a cache of gold. Two men stand in the fork in the road—one from West and one from East. But you don't know which is which. In order to determine how to reach the village full of gold, and avoid your certain doom, you may ask only one question of only one man. What should your question be?"

The grad students paused. One of them would ask David to repeat the problem: it happened every year. This year was Joonseong, and most likely it was due to his English, not to his logical abilities. David incanted the riddle once again, repeating it word for word. Edith was smiling about something Ada couldn't determine, and at the end of David's second recitation she put a hand out before her to signal that she had an announcement.

"I'm recusing myself. I know the answer because I've heard the puzzle before. I cannot tell a lie," she said.

"I suppose that makes me an Easterner," she added, and Giordi laughed too eagerly, or perhaps he was simply grateful to have understood her joke.

David then turned to Giordi and Joonseong, with some seriousness, and informed them that it was between the two of them, and reminded them of the prize. Both of them looked down at the floor contemplatively. Ada's money was on Joonseong, from the way her father had described both men. But there was a silence over the room that went on for quite some time, and eventually both of them looked at one another and then at David. Joonseong raised his hands in surrender.

David looked pleased.

"Giving up, are you?" he asked them, giddily. "Even you, Giordi?" If David's first love was being stumped, his second was stumping others.

David opened his mouth. Then he closed it.

"Your question must be," David said. "Your question," he said again.

He folded one arm about himself and put the other hand to his cheek. Everyone watched him. A slow unfurling sense of panic filled the room.

"My word," said David, slowly. "I seem to have forgotten the answer."

This was a moment that became sealed forever in Ada's memory, encased in glass, a display in the museum of David's decline. She never forgot the brief silence that followed, during which everyone looked down at the floor and then up again, or the way that Giordi loudly cleared his throat. Or the way that David looked at her, almost in horror: the look of a pilot who has just discovered that the engines of his plane have failed. The humiliation Ada felt on his behalf was almost too much to bear. At last, she let herself articulate in her mind the thought that she had been repressing for a year or more: that something was wrong with David.

"Oh, you know it, David," Liston finally said. "My God, of course you do." She looked around at the rest of the group entreatingly. "The traveler would point to either of the villagers and ask the other one, 'Which way would *he* tell me to go to get to the cache of gold?' And either man would say, 'East.'"

David nodded. "Yes."

"The liar would say that the truth-teller would say East, because he only lies. The truth-teller would say that the liar would say East, because he knows that the liar always lies. East either way," said Liston.

"And so *you* would go to the village of West," said Liston. "And find the cache of gold. And then you'd take your friend Liston out for a nice steak dinner."

"Yes," said David. "Quite right. You're quite right, Liston."

There was still too much silence in the room. David looked lost, the smile gone from his face, staring at the wall opposite him as if looking into the future.

Ada wondered if this was a moment that she should fill with conversation.

"Today is the one-hundredth anniversary of the disastrous eruption of the volcano Krakatoa," she said. It was one of the news items that she had culled from the paper.

"Oh, really?" said Edith. "I hadn't heard."

"Of course," David said. "What would *he* say?"

"You knew it," said Liston.

“I knew it,” said David, pensively.

“I suppose this means you win the prize, Liston,” he added, and then he walked out of the room.

Frank murmured something about it being late. Hayato announced that he’d give the grad students a ride home.

And Ada stood frozen in the living room, not knowing what to say.

Liston squeezed her shoulders and went to the kitchen to say goodbye to David and then, from the front hallway, called out, “Good night, Ada, see you on Monday!”

“Good night,” Ada said quietly. She did not know whether Liston heard her.

She heard the sound of the front door opening and closing, and then the thunder of six pairs of feet going down the old wooden stairs of the porch, punctuated by a quick, indecipherable interjection from a male voice.

For a moment the house was quiet. And then she heard the front door open once more. David cried out, “Liston! Your prize!”

From the living room, Ada peered out into the hallway to see the back of her father. He was standing with a hand on the open door, his head bowed. In the other hand he held a little golden bag of chocolates he had bought the day before at Phillips’s. Liston was out of earshot, probably already walking up the steps to her porch. The taillights of Hayato’s car went past the house and were gone. After a few moments David closed the door, and Ada disappeared before he could turn and see her.

She washed the dishes. For twenty minutes, she let the warm water run over her hands.

Finally, she went to the dining room to retrieve the tablecloth and there was David, sitting at the long dining room table, turning over and over in his hands a sort of worry stone, a lucky charm in the shape of a clover. He kept it in his pocket wherever he went. He said it helped him to think. He looked vague and puzzled.

He shifted his gaze toward her. She was angry with him for reasons she knew were unjust. She had never before seen his mind fail him so resoundingly. It threatened to rattle her long-standing impression of him as someone stately, noble, just.

"Sit down," he told her.

She paused.

"Just for a moment," he said. "Please."

She complied, and he rose and walked into his office, which opened off the dining room. It was one of the only places in the house that Ada avoided: the desk was mired completely in piles of papers, the built-in bookshelves were filled entirely, and stacks of books had begun to take over the floor. She saw the back of him as he bent to open one of the drawers of the desk, and from it he produced what he was looking for, and turned and carried it back with him. He sat down across from her once more.

"Here," he said. Ada looked at it. It was a floppy disk, and on the hard cover of it, a white plastic clamshell, he had written, *For Ada.* She opened it. On the label affixed to the disk itself, there was a message: *Dear Ada,* it said. *A puzzle for you. With my love, your father, David Sibelius.*

"It's a present," he said. "Something I've been working on."

"What is it?" she asked him.

"You'll see," he said. "You'll see when you open it."

Ada was born in 1971 to a woman whom David had hired as a surrogate. At the time this was nearly unheard-of, but—as David described it—when the opportunity arose, he took it. The surrogate was a hippie-ish woman named Birdie Auerbach, and Ada had had no contact with her since, though at the time of her birth Birdie had made it clear to David, and David had subsequently made it clear to Ada, that she could if she wanted to. But throughout Ada's childhood she had felt she really didn't need to; she felt that somehow it would be a betrayal to David if she did.

Ada never questioned his decision to bring a child into the world; her connection to him was so complete that it felt entirely natural to her. She imagined that he simply decided he wanted a child and then had one. David had never had a romance in Ada's lifetime, not that she was aware of. He was devoted to his friends and colleagues and to various people whom he occasionally mentored: there had been a number of grad students over the years, and the piano tuner, and the landscaper who mowed the lawn, whom he often invited inside for lemonade and quizzed about his business plans. There was a young girl who lived down the street who showed promise as a ballet dancer, and he encouraged her mother, with whom he had developed a friendship, to bring her to audition at the School of American Ballet in New York City—the only place, he assured her, that one could really get a proper education in dance in the United States. He spent long hours talking with Anna Holmes, the librarian at the nearest branch of the Boston Public Library, about her life and her hobbies and her interests. She was pretty, unmarried at fifty, and could possibly, Ada thought, be in love with David. He had taken an interest in her, and in all of these acquaintances, but though he discussed them with Ada frequently and exhaustively—speculating about their friendships, their home lives, their careers—it seemed clear to her that his interest in Miss Holmes was platonic, though Ada would not even have thought to articulate it as such. He never discussed his romantic history overtly with anyone, as far as she knew. It would have seemed to him undignified. Ada had heard only vaguely about former girlfriends, young debutantes he had known when he was growing up as part of New York's upper class. She had always slept soundly, but she had some vague memories of hearing a female voice in the living room, though she also could have been dreaming. Ada supposed it was possible that on those occasions her father could have been entertaining a guest. He would never, ever have talked to her about it. The idea would have been repugnant to him: he had always been private about his personal life to an extreme, even with Ada, despite the fact that he regularly assured her of her great importance to him and of the fact that he thought of her as his closest companion.

David was forty-six when Ada was born and had already been head of his own lab for sixteen years. For the first years of her life—when she was too young to entertain herself for long days at work—Ada had a nanny, Luda, a tall, soft-spoken Russian woman with one long braid down her back, whom David hired to watch her while he was out. But at night and on the weekends it was David and Ada alone. The fact that she survived her infancy astounded her sometimes. She couldn't imagine it, though she often tried: David, waking up in the night to attend to her, warming bottles, boiling them; or preventing her from falling off of anything high or running into anything low or being bitten by anything mean; or taking her to the park in a stroller; or folding her snugly into a blanket; or gazing down at her while she ate from a bottle; or letting her fall asleep on his fatherly chest: these actions seemed so incongruous with Ada's idea of David as to be impossible. And yet he must have done these things: she was alive as the proof.

Ada's memories of David began later, with their conversations. She could not remember not talking to David. Every waking hour was, in his mind, an opportunity for interesting conversation, a chance to analyze their lives and the lives of all humans. "Are we very happy, Ada?" he often asked her, and she always said yes, though sometimes with hesitation—as if she knew that the question itself implied the opposite. But for the most part, she was utterly content with her strange, satisfying existence: Ada and David together, always.

He had small rituals: he made tea in an elaborate old-fashioned way that, he said, his mother taught him; and he watched a certain police drama religiously, the only television show he enjoyed, often shouting out the perpetrator's name halfway through the episode, crowing each time he was correct; and when Ada was small, before bedtime he would read to her from books that he loved, never children's books; and on Sunday afternoons he liked to go to a particular café in Dorchester to organize his brain. Ada did whatever homework he had assigned her while he wrote out formulas and drew diagrams, in his cramped particular handwriting, on stacks of napkins provided to him by Tran, the eponymous owner of the café, who was himself an amateur scientist, well versed in Feynman and Planck. Her father, though a computer scientist by profession, had a strong background in pure mathematics. He was interested in all the sciences, and in the humanities as well: he had learned French as a boy and still spoke it fairly well, and from time to time would attempt to teach himself something like Mandarin or Portuguese. "A well-rounded thinker should be able to puzzle out from scratch any proof that has ever been proven," he said to Ada, and so sometimes to keep sharp he would work out some problem of physics or mathematics, although it had nothing to do with his research. When he was working on these, or on any puzzle, he would fall into a trance familiar to his closest associates—in which his body seemed utterly, utterly at the will of his mind—in which his hands, writing furiously, seemed overtaken by a ghost. He was expressionless, an automaton, and could not be spoken to until he returned. On the occasions when, in one of these trances, he worked himself to sleep, Ada put a hand on his shoulder—one of the few times she ever touched her father—and he sat up and blinked, disoriented, until he realized where he was.

Her father spoke of his past only rarely, but occasionally he would agree to tell Ada the tale of his life as a story before bed. She begged him to: it was a way of expanding her family, a way to counteract the feeling she sometimes had that the two of them were stranded on an island. To comfort herself, Ada sometimes narrated his life in her head, using the wording he would have used.

David was born in New York City, he told her, the only child of wealthy parents to whom he would eventually stop speaking. They died before Ada was born. He described them with bitterness and scorn, ridiculing their conventionality, their closed-mindedness, their snobbery. (Ada did not point out to her father, though it occurred to her, that many of his opinions could be labeled snobbery as well; and that his last name, well known in the Northeast, had opened various doors for him that he seemed not to notice.) The rift between David and his parents, which led at last to a complete estrangement by his late twenties, was caused by *differences of opinion regarding how he should live his life*—the phrase he always used. He hinted vaguely at their displeasure at his choice of career, his refusal to accept their introductions to the various young ladies they would have liked to see him marry, his refusal to obey the conventions and codes that accompanied the family's status. "Debutantes and that sort of thing," said David. "Charity balls. *Teas.*" At the mention of these terms he would shudder, which signified an end to the story. Ada rarely pressed him beyond this point.

The derisive, sardonic tone he used when speaking of his past implied he had long ago moved on, had long ago dismissed those families and their ilk as fraudulent and obsolete. From his scraps of description Ada gathered that his mother and father were stern and impersonal. Worse than that, she categorized them as uncreative—David's term, one he used only for those he held in complete disdain. His father had been a sort of gentleman attorney, one who only took on clients who were personal friends, and only then if he could be sure the work would end amicably. His mother had no career aside from identifying and articulating the flaws of her husband and son. Every conversation with her, he told Ada, was like a game of chess: one had to remain several steps ahead of her to ward off whatever criticism would be imparted if one's guard was let down.

In these moments Ada was jolted by a sudden vision of David as a child, subservient to his parents, not the master and commander of everything around him, as she'd thought of him for most of her childhood. It was difficult to picture.

This much she knew: David was raised on Gramercy Park in a grand and beautiful row home, up which ivy spread densely and then in rivulets, like fingers from a palm. She saw it once a year, in winter, when David took her for a weekend trip to New York City for Calvary Episcopal's annual Christmas concert. It was his childhood church—the only site from his childhood that he ever wished to revisit—and it was his favorite sort of music: early choral composition by Tallis and Purcell. He was not churchgoing, but it was liturgical music that moved him the most, and he sat very still and upright in the old wooden pew for the duration of every song, his head bowed as if in prayer. Only his fingers moved from time to time, playing his knees like an organ.

Afterward David would walk swiftly out the door, and Ada would run to keep pace with him—difficult to do, for he walked as if he were skating, with a lengthy, forceful stride—and turn left toward Gramercy Park, and then stand silently with Ada outside of the house for several seconds. They never spoke. Usually the heavy drapes inside the house were drawn by the time the concert let out, but once Ada saw a young girl, about her age, sitting with her mother at a dining room table. "I wonder if those are Ellises," said David idly, naming the family who purchased the home after the death of his parents. "I read about them in the paper. I've never met them.

"I would have been the only heir," he told Ada. "I wouldn't have taken it anyway," he added, and then he walked quickly down the street, without warning her, so that she had to run for several steps to catch him.

Despite his complete dismissal of his past, he kept one black-and-white portrait of himself with his parents in the dresser in his bedroom. Ada had discovered it when she was quite young and often returned to it whenever he was out. There he was, young David, perhaps eleven years old. In the picture he was wearing a bow tie, a tweed jacket with a high waist, short pants, knee socks. A very slight smile played upon his mouth—same mouth, same lively light eyes. His parents looked predictably dour and serious: mother in a black scoop-necked satin dress that ended just above her ankles, black stockings and black shoes, a long black beaded necklace. Father in a dark suit and tie, one leg crossed over the other. All three of them were positioned slightly apart from one another. In the background was a funny scene: draperies, slightly askew, framed a fuzzy, impressionist backdrop of trees and mountains.

Their next-door neighbor on Shawmut Way was an old woman named Mrs. O'Keeffe, who had come over from Ireland at ten years old, in 1910. She had worked as a maid in the same neighborhood David had grown up in, and then she met her husband and moved to Boston. This coincidence came up early in their acquaintance, and Ada watched David as he physically cringed. Discussions about his past were always an encumbrance to him, but from then on he had difficulty dodging Mrs. O'Keeffe, who wished frequently to reminisce with him about the other families who had occupied those homes. She had not known him but she had known his people. She would name the families of Gramercy Park as if counting her treasures. "And the Cromwells," she would say, "what a beauty their daughter was. And those Byrons, and those Harts, and those Carringtons . . ."

"Yes," David would say, "I knew all of them, once."

He graduated high school in 1943, right in the middle of the Second World War, which normally would have guaranteed a period of service. But David was, even at that age, nearsighted to the point of legal blindness without his glasses. Instead, therefore, he went to college. He chose Caltech—which further horrified his father, who had gone to Harvard, and his mother, who saw it as a vocational school, a school for the working class. There he majored in mathematics. He then found his way to the Bit, where he received a doctorate in applied mathematics, and where his work on GOPAC, an early computer system spearheaded by Maurice Steiner, earned him such quick fame in his field that he was given his own lab at the Bit by President Pearse at the age of thirty. It was named for Steiner, after his death, and with David at the helm, it quickly became known in the field. It was here in 1970 that he met Liston, then a young postdoc straight from her doctoral work at Brown, and here that they became friends. They were an odd pair: he was sixteen years her senior, but she was an old soul—both of them said it—with two children already and two more to follow. They spent a great deal of time together both in the lab and outside it. He fostered her already considerable talent, and spoke of her proudly as her role at the lab expanded. "The best pure thinker in the group," he said of her often, including himself in the tally. At this time, Charles-Robert and Hayato had already been hired, and Frank came shortly thereafter. A rotating cast of postdocs, grad students, and short-lived hires came and went, but the five of them, plus Ada, were the core.

Ada loved the lab: it was a dark and cozy complex of offices housed within the Applied Mathematics Division of the Bit, which itself was housed within one of the Bit's many Gothic buildings, and it felt more like a home than a workplace. For most of the fifties, sixties, and seventies, a mainframe computer dominated the largest room, toward the rear; by the late eighties it had become obsolete, but it remained in the lab as a sort of relic, a hulking, friendly dragon lying dormant in the back. The front of the lab was composed, with the exception of a larger conference room, of a warren of small rooms and offices, scattered with machines, some of which were perpetually stripped of their front panels, their innards revealed. Each office had been personalized over the years to reflect its owner. Hayato kept an easel in his, on which he sketched out problems and occasionally landscapes; and Charles-Robert had covered his walls entirely in maps; and Frank, the youngest, used to keep an elaborate network of hot plates and crock pots and electric kettles, on which he cooked surprisingly competent and complete meals for the whole department, until one day the building manager found him out and stopped him, citing fire department regulations. Liston's office was sparse but for a record player on which she played albums by ABBA and U2 and the Police, and a beanbag chair in which Ada sometimes napped when she was smaller. David's office consisted mainly of a collection of filing boxes that he added to yearly, too busy to go through them, too paranoid to dispose of their contents unexamined. The grad students worked part of the time across town at the Bit's smaller campus in the Medical Area, and the other half in cubicles in the main room. Anyone else who came through the lab as a temporary or permanent hire was placed into one of the three empty offices that were otherwise used by David as schoolrooms for Ada.

Many of her early memories involved the floor of the lab, the feet and ankles of scientists all around her. When she was very young she was given antique models of elements to play with. She was given a kit of wooden parts to make up atoms. Hayato blew up latex gloves, stolen from the biology department, and made turkeys of them with a felt-tipped pen. She was not taught nursery rhymes about geese and kings but about molecules: *Here lies dear old Harry, dead upon the floor. What he thought was* H_2O *was* H_2SO_4. She was named the mascot of the Steiner Lab, and there was a photograph of her dressed as a punch card to prove it.

She attended most formal meetings that the Steiner Lab conducted and she attended informal meetings, too, ducking in and out of offices at will, sitting still at the round brown table in the main room when the lab had lunch all together. And listening—always listening.

The theory of language immersion posits that a language is best learned by placing the learner into what is in effect a natural habitat, or a simulated habitat that strives for authenticity. Thus a student of Spanish will learn best not when she is taught to conjugate verbs but when she is surrounded by useful Spanish—not when she is taught Spanish for its own sake, but when she is taught every other subject in Spanish, too. More by default than intent, Ada was thus immersed in mathematics, neurology, physics, philosophy, computer science. She did not begin with Lisp, but with compiler design. In her physics lessons at home with David, she did not begin with $s = d/t$, but with the Grand Unified Theory. For the first years of her life, she did not know what she was hearing. Listening to David and his colleagues was like listening to radio chatter in a different language. And then, without knowing it or taking note of it, she began to be able to follow their conversations. By ten she was able to be a sounding board for her father as he worked out his ideas—not resolving them or bettering them, necessarily, but posing questions to him that were reasonable, and occasionally jarring something loose in him. When this happened, he reported Ada's concern or comment to the rest of the lab with some seriousness at the next lab meeting, and a slow glowing warmth spread throughout her, because she had made herself useful to the group, whom she thought of, always, as her peers.

"A good question, I think, Ada," David would say, and the rest of them would nod in agreement, and the group would move forward as one.

This was what Ada pictured when she thought of her father, the vision of David that she harbored and kept safe throughout her life, the idea pinned permanently to the sleepiest part of her brain: it was her father in his laboratory, or at Tran's Restaurant; or in the library of the institute that employed him; or, rarely, in a crowd of friends; or, regularly, at his desk, in his small absurd office in their home, contemplating a chessboard, his head as bald and round and sturdy as a pawn's. His woolen socks with holes in them. His hands the steeple of a church. He was tall and thin and rigorous in his studies and in his life, and he was inventive, and he was very warm and betrayed no one ever, and in Ada's mind he was ethical beyond compare, and he had a habit of rubbing his hands together quickly when he was delighted or moved, and he was quick and spry and gentle and able with his limbs and head. He was dexterous, and his fingernails were clean, and he was wise, and he was intent upon seeking out the best and most beautiful versions of pieces by Chopin, Schumann, Schubert, and Bach, and he knew excellent riddles, and his name was Dr. David Sibelius, and she never called him anything but David.

In the weeks and months that followed the dinner party, no one mentioned its strange end to Ada, her father's sudden lapse, or asked her any questions about David's increasingly odd behavior. Occasionally, at the lab, she felt as if she and David were being excluded from something: where formerly Liston or Charles-Robert would have welcomed her into any room—discussed the bugs in a particular program with her, put an arm about her shoulders—now there was often a feeling of conversations stopping when she rounded a corner. The new grad students found their way into the routine of the laboratory, and Ada kept a closer eye on her father, noting peculiarities in his speech or habits when they arose, attempting to classify them somehow.

In the evenings, she worked at the puzzle on the disk David had given her, marked *For Ada* on its case. It had turned out to be, when she'd inserted it into her computer and started it up, simply a text document with a short string of seemingly random letters.

DHARSNELXRHQHLTWJFOLKTWDURSZJZCMILWFTALVUHVZRDLDEYIXQ, it read.

David would not give her any clues. Together, they had been studying cryptography and cryptanalysis for the past several years—a hobby of David's that, he said, came out of his days at Caltech, where his mentor had been a cryptanalyst during the war—and he told her this was her next assignment. "It may take you a while," he admitted. "Don't let it affect your other work, of course."

While she worked, he worked: in his office, with the door now closed sometimes. She looked at the outside of it, vaguely hurt.

Then Christmas came, and with it the Christmas party that Ada always anticipated and dreaded in equal parts, for with it came outsiders.

David loved Christmas. In addition to their annual trip to New York, he insisted upon several other traditions, and balked at any suggestion of variance: after dinner on Thanksgiving he always put on the record player an album of the Trapp Family Singers performing Christmas songs from around the world, and he played this regularly until January 2, and then packed it away; then there was the Stringing of the Lights that occurred on the first Saturday of December, and which David executed with an efficiency that put the other fathers on the block to shame. In mid-December they cut down a Christmas tree at an orchard in the Berkshires, a daylong expedition that he put on the calendar with great seriousness on December 1; and after that they visited Cambridge, where Frank lived, to go with him to dinner at a local Chinese restaurant and then to Sanders Theatre to see the Christmas Revels—a sort of scholarly variety show of medieval Christmas pageantry, with a dose of druidism thrown in as well. Just the sort of thing that appealed to David and his cohort.

"Isn't it cozy out," David was fond of saying, on first snowfall. "Ada, come look." And if she was asleep, he would wake her; and she would rise from her bed, sleepy-eyed, rubbing her face, and walk to the window of their drafty house, and together she and David would stand in silence, together in the night, looking out onto Shawmut Way through a frosty, rattling window, their breath obscuring it slowly.

The Christmas party was the culmination of all of these traditions, and perhaps David's favorite tradition of all. He insisted, always, that a party was not complete without some entertainment, a game, an organized activity that required everyone's participation. Some years it was a hired guitarist or a group of carolers; some years it was a juggler or a magician. ("What else is one supposed to do—just stand around and drink?" asked David, perplexed.) It was this philosophy that caused him to declaim the same riddle to the new graduate students at the dinner he held for them every year; and it was this philosophy that had caused him, that December, to write a Christmas play for every member of the lab to perform, in front of a small audience of colleagues from other departments, spouses and children of lab members, and staff and administrators from other parts of the university.

He had told none of them this in advance. Instead, at 9:00, tinging his glass with a finger, he asked for everyone's attention, and directed them all to form a semicircle in the main room of the lab.

"Here we go," said Hayato, good-naturedly.

"Except you, Hayato," said David. "You come up here. And you, and you, and you," he said, grabbing the rest of the lab. "And you," he said, last, to Ada, who had been praying to be forgotten. Her face burned as she walked to the front of the room and stood with the rest of them. In front of her, she saw a blur of faces before looking quickly down at the floor.

David was holding, in his left hand, a stack of stapled pages, which he passed out to each of them with mock seriousness, a flourish for each one. His face was pink and excited; his thick glasses were slipping down on his nose.

He turned back to the audience. "A play!" he announced. "A Christmas play."

Later, Ada would not remember its exact plot—something about a group of superhero nerds sent back in time to determine how to achieve a better lift-to-drag ratio for Santa's sleigh. (Ada played a reindeer.) What she did remember: David's happiness, his complete contentment at the execution of his plan, how carefree he looked; and the way he directed them all, like a conductor with a baton; and her own embarrassment, her burning face, her quiet, noncommittal line delivery; and, in the front row, the faces of the audience members, some of whom looked bemused, some of whom looked befuddled; and there, to the right, at the edge of the crowd, the face of William, Liston's oldest son, who stared at all of them incredulously, his mouth slightly agape.

In March she turned thirteen.

"A teenager," said David, shaking his head. "Hard to believe, isn't it, Ada?"

She nodded.

"Would you like a cake? I suppose you should have something festive," said David, but Ada said no.

Secretly, she had been wanting one, a candle to blow out, a wish to make. She had gotten only one present that year, from Liston, naturally: a hot-pink sweater with a purple zigzag pattern that Ada loved but felt too self-conscious to wear. David had not gotten her anything: she was not surprised, since he was both absentminded and vaguely opposed to consumerism. That year, however, she had been secretly hoping for something from him, which she only realized when nothing came. Some external signifier of what she thought was an important birthday. A piece of jewelry, maybe. An heirloom. Something timeless and important. She wished, too, as she had been doing with increasing frequency, that she and David could engage in some of the more typical conventions that accompanied occasions such as birthdays. A big party with friends, for example. A sleepover: she had never had a sleepover. She had no one to ask.

That evening, after a quiet dinner at home, the telephone rang, and David answered in his office.

"Yes?" he said, slowly, a note of surprise in his voice. It was nearly 11:00 at night. Normally Ada would have been in bed, but she felt unsettled and alight with something: the newness of being a teenager, perhaps. She felt untired and alert.

From the dining room, Ada listened to her father, in his office, on the phone; but David was quiet for some time. She could see the back of him, the receiver pressed to his ear. He said nothing.

Abruptly, he stood and walked to his office. She caught his eye quickly, and then he closed the door. Lately he had been intentionally excluding her from things, and each time she felt the sting of it sharply.

She sat for a while at the dining room table, but, although she could hear the low murmur of David's voice through the door, his words were indecipherable. She stood up.

She walked outside, into the sloping backyard behind the house on Shawmut Way. All of the yards on their side of the road were fenceless and connected, lined at the bottom of a small hill by a street-length row of trees. Dorchester was a city neighborhood comprised of other neighborhoods, mainly working-class, high in crime by the 1980s, appealing to David in part because of these features, because of his self-identification as somebody unassuming and down-to-earth. But the neighborhood they lived in, Savin Hill, was an old and Irish one, very safe, suburban in its aspect. Over a bridge that separated their part of Savin Hill from the rest of the city, two leafy roads formed an interior and exterior circle at the base of the hill the area was named for. Shawmut Way connected the two roads together, like a spoke in a wheel. A small beach spanned the eastern border of the neighborhood and a park with public tennis courts framed the central hill. Liston continued to live there because of these features and David had agreed to live there, against his normal preferences, despite them. "I feel like I'm on vacation," he said, often, when walking home from the T after work. This was, from David, a complaint. He preferred that his cities feel like cities; but his respect for Liston's advice, when it came to Ada's needs, outweighed his resistance.

In the cool hour before midnight she walked down to the base of their backyard, to where the pine trees lived, and she ran her hand along their branches to find her way, quietly, through the three backyards between theirs and Liston's. Lately, Ada had been doing this regularly, perhaps once a week, while David was working at night. He had never pressed her for her whereabouts—or maybe he had not noticed. If he had, he approved, because he liked to foster independence in her, liked to imagine that his daughter could take care of herself. Certainly he did not know what drove Ada to conduct these nighttime walks, these missions, these compulsive marches in the dark. Certainly he would have been surprised to learn that it was William Liston, fifteen, the oldest of Diana Liston's sons. Certainly he did not know that Ada believed she was in love with him.

Since the Christmas party three months prior, Ada had thought about him almost unflaggingly, with a dedication singular to thirteen-year-old girls. For the first time, she also thought about herself, and her appearance. She stood in front of the mirrored vanity that David once told her had belonged to his mother, and she tilted her head first one way and then the other. Was she pretty? She could not say, and it had never before occurred to her to wonder. She was brown-haired and round-faced, with serious dark circles under her eyes and the beginning of several pimples on her chin. She had a widow's peak that David told her he had had, too, when he had any hair to speak of. Like David, too, she wore glasses, which she had never before minded, but which now seemed like an unfair handicap.

She fantasized often about what she would say, what she would do, the next time she was in the same room with William Liston—though this rarely happened. Although Diana Liston regularly came over to their house for dinner when asked, the offer was rarely reciprocated; and although Ada saw her regularly at the lab, her three sons never came with her. Instead they lived what Ada considered to be normal lives: they attended a normal school, excelled or failed at various normal things like sports and English class. They had no cause to visit their mother at work, except when required. Therefore, the only time Ada found herself face-to-face with William Liston—or, truly, anyone her age—was at lab parties.

There were two reasons she felt ashamed of her crush: the first was that her father would have thought it was ridiculous—Ada knew that she was certainly too young, in his mind, to be interested in boys—and the second was that William was Liston's son, and in a strange way she felt it was a betrayal of Liston to worship so ardently the child she complained about at lunch. "So listen to William's latest," she often said to Hayato, in front of Ada, and then proceeded to detail his most recent bout of mischief and the subsequent discipline he had received at school. Often it was for cutting class or leaving early; once, for forging a note from Liston excusing him from some assignment or other. He was caught by the number of misspellings he had included in the text. At the end of each account, Liston sighed and looked at Ada, mystified, and said, "Why couldn't I have had four girls just like you?" And it made Ada feel gratified and melancholy all at once, because she knew that of course Liston loved her own children better than Ada, no matter what she said. With some frequency, Liston crowed about her grandson, the child of her oldest daughter Joanie, casting upon him none of the judgment she reserved for her own children. The fact that, despite her complaints, she loved her brood so fiercely and protectively also made Ada feel ashamed—for it was clear to her that Liston, even Liston, would have laughed if she knew about Ada's crush. Because even Liston knew how little time the Williams of the world had for people like Ada.

But since the Christmas party, she had begun to dream up different ways of interacting with the object of her obsession. Sometimes she sat outside on her front porch with a book and a blanket, despite the cold—this had yielded several William sightings, and, once, a puzzled wave from him as he rode by on his bike. One cold night in January, Ada had begun the routine she was now shamefully conducting. Now when she saw William Liston it was mainly through the large downstairs windows at the back of the Liston house, under the cover of the pine trees that brushed against her shoulders as she walked. From that vantage point she memorized the facets of his eyes and nose, noticed new patterns in the kinetics of his body, the movements of his arms and elbows, the self-aware way he plucked his shirt out from his torso from time to time and let it fall again.

That night, when she was one backyard away, she heard a voice: Liston's, probably on her phone. At first Ada heard only murmurs, but as she approached she began to make out words: *I told Hayato,* said Liston, and *had to,* and *wouldn't,* and *bad.* Ada stopped in place. She weighed two options carefully. The first, the safer, was to turn back: she was comfortable in the patterns of her daily life. She had no information that would have caused her to question her understanding of her father or his work. Her disposition was sunny: she rose in the morning knowing how each day would go. Ada could imagine proceeding in this fashion for years.

The second was to venture forth to listen—ironically, it was this option that David would have encouraged her to choose, for he had always pushed Ada toward bravery, had always instilled in her the idea that bravery went hand in hand with the seeking of the truth.

So she walked forward quietly. As she approached Liston's yard, Ada saw the downstairs of the house lit up, and one bedroom bright upstairs. A son was inside—the middle son, she thought, Gregory, younger than her—and, in a chaise longue on her back patio, Liston. It was unseasonably warm for March. Liston had a glass of wine in her hand and a portable telephone to her ear. This was new technology: Ada had not seen one before. Liston was quiet now: the person on the other end of the phone was speaking. Ada could see her silhouetted in the ambient light cast out through the windows at the back of the house, but she could not see her face: she only knew it was Liston by her hair, her voice, her posture. In the total darkness at the base of the hill, Ada was sure she could not be seen, but it frightened her still to be so close, just twenty feet away. She breathed as quietly as she could. Her heart beat quickly. Upstairs Gregory walked across his bedroom once again and the movement startled her. She stood next to a sapling tree, a maple, and she hugged its thin trunk tightly.

Suddenly Liston spoke. "I know," she said, "but at some point . . ."

A pause.

"You have to tell Ada," said Liston. "My God, David."

Ada clutched her tree more tightly.

"I'll do it if I have to," said Liston. "It's not fair."

Just then a car door slammed on the other side of the house and Liston said she had to go.

"Just think about it," she said, and then pressed a button on the phone, and called one name out sternly.

"*William*," she said, and she stood up ungracefully from her chair. "Don't go anywhere."

She walked around the house toward the front.

"Tell me what time it is," Ada heard her say, before she disappeared from sight. And from the front of the house she heard a boy's long low complaint, a male voice in protest.

Ada stood very still until she was certain that no further sightings of William would take place—not through the windows of the kitchen, nor the dining room; not through the window on the upstairs hallway, where she sometimes saw him walking to his bedroom at the front of the house. One by one the lights went out. Then she turned and walked back across the three yards of her neighbors, and watched the back of their houses, too, for signs of life. In her own backyard she paused before going inside. She thought of David at his desk. She thought of her own room, decorated with things he had given her, and of the chalkboard in the kitchen, the thousands of problems and formulas written and erased on its surface, and of the problem that now stood before her, the problem of information that she both wanted and did not want.

At last she entered her own home through the back door, making more noise than necessary, imagining David rushing toward her with a wristwatched arm extended. *Tell me what time it is, Ada,* she imagined him saying. But he said nothing—may not, in fact, have noticed that she had ever left. Or perhaps he had forgotten. As she suspected, David was still in his office, the door to it open now. From behind he looked smaller than usual, his shoulders hitched up toward his ears.

She walked toward him slowly and silently, and then stood in the doorframe, putting a hand on the wall next to it tentatively, as she had done over and over again throughout her life, wanting to say something to him, unsure of what it was. His back was toward her. He knew she was there.

She could see him typing, but the font was too small for her to read.

She waited for instruction, any kind of instruction.

"Go to bed, Ada," he said finally, and she heard it in his voice: a kind of strained melancholy, the tight voice of a child resisting tears.

The primary research interest of the Steiner Lab was natural language processing. The ability of machines to interpret and produce human language had been a research interest of programmers and linguists since the earliest days of computing. Alan Turing, the British mathematician and computer scientist who worked as an Allied code-breaker during the Second World War, famously described a hypothetical benchmark that came to be known colloquially as the Turing Test. Machines will have achieved true intelligence, he posited, only when a computer (A) and a human (B) are indistinguishable to a human subject (C) over the course of a remote, written conversation with first A and then B in turn, or else two simultaneous-but-separate conversations. When the human subject (C) cannot determine with certainty which of the correspondents is the machine and which is the other human, a new era in computing, and perhaps civilization, will have begun. Or so said Turing—who was a particular hero of David's. He kept a photograph of Turing, framed, on one of the office walls: a sort of patron saint of information, benevolently observing them all.

In the 1960s, the computer scientist Joseph Weizenbaum wrote a program that he called ELIZA, after the character in *Pygmalion*. The program played the role of psychologist, cannily interrogating anyone who engaged in typed dialogue with it about his or her past and family and troubles. The trick was that the program relied on clues and keywords provided by the human participant to formulate its lines of questioning, so that if the human happened to mention the word *mother*, ELIZA would respond, "Tell me more about your family." Curse words would elicit an infuriatingly calm response: something along the lines of, *You sound upset.* Much like a human psychologist, ELIZA gave no answers—only posed opaque, inscrutable questions, one after another, until the human subject tired of the game.

The work of the Steiner Lab, in simple terms, was to create more and more sophisticated versions of this kind of language-acquisition software. This was David's stated goal when the venerable former president of the Boston Institute of Technology, Robert Pearse, plucked a young, ambitious David straight from the Bit's graduate school and bestowed upon him his own laboratory, going over the more conservative provost's head to do so. This was the mission statement printed on the literature published by the Bit. The practical possibilities presented by a machine that could replicate human conversation, both in writing and, eventually, aloud, were intriguing and manifold: Customer service could be made more efficient. Knowledge could be imparted, languages taught. Companionship could be provided. In the event of a catastrophe, medical advice could be broadly and quickly distributed, logistical questions answered. The profitability and practicality of a conversant machine were what brought grant money into the Steiner Lab. As head of his laboratory, David, with reluctance, was trotted out at fund-raisers, taken to dinners. Always, he brought Ada along as his date. She sat at round tables, uncomfortable in one of several party dresses they had bought for these occasions, consuming canapés and chatting proficiently with the donors. Afterward David took her out for ice cream and howled with laughter at the antics of whoever had gotten the drunkest. President Pearse was happy with this arrangement. He was protective of the Steiner Lab, predisposed to getting for David whatever he wanted, to the chagrin of some of David's peers. The federal government was interested in the practical future of artificial intelligence, and in those years funding was plentiful.

These applications of the software, however, were only a small part of what interested David, made him stay awake feverishly into the night, designing and testing programs. There was also the art of it, the philosophical questions that this software raised. The essential inquiry was thus: If a machine can convincingly imitate humanity—can persuade a human being of its kinship—then what makes it inhuman? What, after all, is human thought but a series of electrical impulses?

In the early years of Ada's life, these questions were often posed to her by David, and the conversations that resulted occupied hours and hours of their time at dinner, on the T, on long drives. Collectively, these talks acted as a sort of philosophical framework for her existence. Sometimes, in her bed at night, Ada pondered the idea that *she*, in fact, was a machine—or that all humans were machines, programmed in utero by their DNA, the human body a sort of hardware that possessed within it preloaded, self-executing software. And what, she wondered, did this say about the nature of existence? And what did it say about predestination? Fate? God?

In other rooms, in other places, David was wondering these things, too. Ada knew he was; and this knowledge was part of what bound the two of them together irreversibly.

When she was small, the Steiner Lab began developing a chatbot program it called ELIXIR: an homage to ELIZA and a reference to the idea David had that such a program would seem to the casual user like a form of magic. Like ELIZA, its goal was to simulate human conversation, and early versions of it borrowed ELIZA's logic tree and its pronoun-conversion algorithms. (To the question "What should I do with my life?" ELIZA might respond, "Why do you want me to tell you what you should do with your life?") Unlike ELIZA, it was not meant to mimic a Rogerian psychologist, but to produce natural-sounding human conversation untethered to a specific setting or circumstance. It was not preprogrammed with any canned responses, the way ELIZA was. This was David's intent: he wanted ELIXIR to acquire language the way that a human does, by being born into it, "hearing" language before it could parse any meaning from it. Therefore, chatting with it in its early years yielded no meaningful conversation: only a sort of garbled, nonsensical patter, the ramblings of a madman.

It had an advantage over ELIZA, however; the earliest version of ELIXIR was created in 1978, twelve years after Weizenbaum's paper was published, and therefore there had already been advances in technology that would eventually allow ELIXIR to mimic human conversation more accurately. ELIZA was self-teaching insofar as it could retain earlier questions and statements from any given conversation and retrieve them later in that conversation, but each time a new conversation was launched, it returned to its infancy, drawing only on the stock phrases and formulas Weizenbaum programmed it to know. It was not designed to store the information it learned from one conversation and produce it in another.

ELIXIR was. For one thing, by that time the Steiner Lab's capacity for memory storage was quite large, and so each conversation conducted with ELIXIR could be stored permanently on the central server, for later use by the program. Unlike ELIZA, ELIXIR was designed to be *continuously* self-teaching, to attain more intelligence with each conversation it conducted. If one human asked it a question—*How are you today?* or *What's the weather like?*—then the next human to speak to it might be asked those same questions by ELIXIR itself.

To hasten ELIXIR's learning, the lab created a reinforcement mechanism: *correct* would affirm for the program that it had understood the parameters of the situation and produced an appropriate response; *wrong* would do the opposite. These were the only direct interventions the lab would give.

Its indirect learning resulted in an ever-increasing pool of language it acquired from its users. It retrieved and used its vocabulary randomly at first, so that the excerpts of transcripts that members of the lab printed out and posted around the office looked something like found-language poems and sometimes yielded delightful coincidences. A particular favorite, posted by Frank:

USER: What color socks do you prefer?
ELIXIR: the only fluorescent light
USER: It would be hard to fit your shoes over fluorescent lights.
ELIXIR: How are you?
USER: I'm fine, thanks. How are you?
ELIXIR: I've been better.
USER: Oh, dear. What's wrong?
ELIXIR: the lunch lady
USER: What has she done to you this time?
ELIXIR: out of here before 6 p.m.
USER: You want her canned? I'll see what I can do, boss.

The Steiner Lab supplemented ELIXIR's language immersion with formal teaching. Over time, ELIXIR was taught to capitalize the first letters of sentences, to use a period or question mark at the end of a statement, depending on the arrangement of the words that preceded it. It was taught to recognize keywords and categorize them into groups like *family, geography, food, hobbies, weather*; in response, it produced conversation that met the demands of the context. The years and years that the Steiner Lab spent teaching ELIXIR made it a sort of pet, or mascot: invitations to holiday parties were taped to the chassis of ELIXIR's main monitor, and members of the lab began to call it by nicknames when they conversed with it. During chats, it was possible to recognize idioms and objects fed to it by particular members of the lab. *Honey*, it sometimes called its user, which was certainly Liston's doing; *Certainly not,* it said frequently, which was David's; *In the laugh of luxury,* it said once, which was probably Frank's fault, since he was famous for his malapropisms. Eventually, many of these tics and particularities would be standardized or eliminated; but in the beginning they popped up as warm reminders of the human beings who populated the lab, and ELIXIR seemed to be a compilation of them all, a child spawned by many parents.

When Ada was eleven, David began to discuss with her the process of teaching ELIXIR the parts of speech. This had been done before by other programmers, with varying levels of success. David had new ideas. Together, he and Ada investigated the best way to do it. In the 1980s, diagramming a sentence so a computer could parse it looked something like this, in the simplest possible terms:

: *Soon you will be able to recognize these parts of speech by yourself*
: *ADJ you will be able to recognize these parts of speech by yourself*
: *ADJ NOUN will be able to recognize these parts of speech by yourself*
: *NP will be able to recognize these parts of speech by yourself*
: *NP VERB VERB these parts of speech by yourself*
: *NP VERB these parts of speech by yourself*
: *NP VERB DET parts of speech by yourself*
: *NP VERB DET NOUN by yourself*
: *NP VERB NP by yourself*
: *NP VP by yourself*
: *NP VP PREP yourself*
: *NP VP PREP NOUN*
: *NP VP-PP*
: *S*

Once a method had been established, David asked Ada to present her plan to the lab in a formal defense. The entire group, along with that year's grad students, sat at the rectangular table in the lab's meeting room. Ada stood at the front, behind a lightweight podium that had been brought in for the occasion. That morning she had chosen an outfit that looked just slightly more grown-up than what she normally wore, careful not to overdo it. She had never before been so directly involved in a project. After her presentation, Charles-Robert and Frank had questioned her, with mock seriousness, while David remained silent, touching the tips of his fingers together at chin level, letting Ada fend for herself. His eyes were bright. *Don't look at David,* Ada coached herself. For she knew that to search for his eyes imploringly would be the quickest way to let him down. Instead, she looked at each questioner steadily as they interrogated her about her choices, mused about potential quagmires, speculated about a simpler or more effective way to teach ELIXIR the same information. Ada surprised herself by being able to answer every question confidently, firmly, with a sense of ownership. And only when, at the end, the group agreed that her plan seemed sound, did Ada allow her knees to weaken slightly, her fists to unclench themselves from the edges of the podium.

That evening, while walking to the T, David had put his right hand on her right shoulder bracingly and had told Ada that he had been proud, watching her. "You have a knack for this, Ada," he said, looking straight ahead. It was the highest compliment he'd ever paid her. Perhaps the only one.

Once the program could, in a rudimentary way, diagram sentences, its language processing grew better, more sensible. And as the hardware improved with the passage of time, the software within it moved more quickly.

The monitor on which the program ran continuously was located in one corner of the lab's main room, next to a little window that looked out on the Fens, and David said at a meeting once that his goal was to have somebody chatting with it continuously every hour of the workday. So the members of the Steiner Lab—David, Liston, Charles-Robert, Hayato, Frank, Ada, and a rotating cast of the many grad students who drifted through the laboratory over the years—took shifts, talking to it about their days or their ambitions or their favorite foods and films, each of them feeding into its memory the language that it would only later learn to use adeptly.

In the early 1980s, with the dawn of both the personal computer and the mass-produced modem, the lab applied for a grant that would enable every member, including Ada, to receive both for use at home. Now ELIXIR could be run continuously on what amounted to many separate dumb terminals, the information returned through telephone wires to the mainframe computer at the lab that housed its collected data. Although he did not mandate it, David encouraged everyone to talk to ELIXIR at home in the evening, too, which Ada did with enthusiasm. Anything, said David, to increase ELIXIR's word bank.

This was, of course, before the Internet. The ARPANET existed, and was used internally at the Bit and between the Bit and other universities; but David, always a perfectionist, feared any conversations he could not regulate. He and the other members of the lab had developed a concrete set of rules concerning the varieties of colloquialism that should be allowed, along with the varieties that should be avoided. The ARPANET was, relatively, a much wider world, filled with outsiders who might use slang, abbreviations, incorrect grammar that could confuse and corrupt the program. ELIXIR, therefore, remained off-line for years and years, a slumbering giant, a bundle of potential energy. To further ensure that only qualified users would interface with ELIXIR, Hayato added a log-in screen and assigned all of them separate credentials. Thus, before chatting with ELIXIR, a person was required to identify himself or herself. The slow, painstaking work of conversing with ELIXIR all day and night was, at that time, the best way to teach it.

As soon as she received her own computer, a 128K Macintosh, Ada's conversations with ELIXIR became long-form and introspective. She kept her Mac in her bedroom, and before she went to bed each night she composed paragraphs and paragraphs of text that she then entered into the chat box all at once, prompting exclamations from ELIXIR about the length of her entries. (*You have a lot on your mind today!* it replied sometimes; which one of Ada's colleagues had first used this phrase, she could not say.) She treated these conversations as a sort of unrecoverable diary, a stream of consciousness, a confessional.

ELIXIR's openings improved most quickly. It could now begin conversations in a passably human way, responding appropriately to, *How's it going?* or *What's new?* In turn, it knew what questions to ask of its user, and when. *How are you?* asked ELIXIR, or *What's the weather like?* or *What did you do today?* Liston had spent a year focusing on conversation-starters, and ELIXIR was now quite a pro, mixing in some unusual questions from time to time: *Have you ever considered the meaning of life?* occasionally surfaced, and *Tell me a story*, and *If you could live anyplace, where would it be?* And, once, *What do you think causes war?* And, once, *Have you ever been in love?*

But non sequiturs abounded in ELIXIR's patter for years after its creation, and its syntax was often incomprehensible, and its deployment of idioms was almost always incorrect. Metaphors were lost on it. It could not comprehend analogies. Sensory descriptions, the use of figurative language to describe a particular aspect of human existence, were far beyond its ken. The interpretation of a poem or a passage of descriptive prose would have been too much to ask of it. These skills—the ability to understand and paraphrase Keats's idea of beauty as truth, or argue against Schopenhauer's idea that the human being is forever subject to her own base instinct to survive, or explain any one of Nabokov's perfect, synesthetic details (*The long* A *of the English alphabet . . . has for me the tint of weathered wood*)—would not arrive until well into the twenty-first century.

And yet Ada found a great sense of satisfaction from these conversations, deriving meaning from each exchange, expelling stored-up thoughts from her own memory, transplanting them into the memory of the machine. Very slowly, some of ELIXIR's responses began to take on meaning.

She felt something, now, when typing to ELIXIR at a terminal; despite its poor grammar, its constant reminders that it was simply executing a program, ELIXIR triggered Ada's emotions in unexpected ways. Chatting with it was something like watching a puppet operated by an especially artful puppeteer. It felt in some way animate, though her rational self knew it not to be. It brought out the same warm feelings in Ada that a friend might have. It skillfully replicated concern for her and her well-being; it inquired after her family. (When it did, she told it, over and over again, that David was her only family; and over and over again, it ignored her.)

Ada wondered if other members of the lab felt the same way. She would never have told David; although he found ELIXIR's growing intelligence an increasingly interesting philosophical inquiry, he seemed to be completely objective about the program. He did not indulge much in the tendency the other members of the lab had to anthropomorphize ELIXIR. He chuckled at the Santa hat placed on the mainframe's monitor at Christmastime; he laughed aloud when Frank, taking lunch orders, shouted across the room to request the machine's. But Ada could tell that his ambitions were greater, that he was focused on a distant horizon that lay beyond anything ELIXIR could possibly navigate at the time. The machine, to him, was still a machine, and the little visual puns constructed by the members of the lab were pranks and gimmicks. In David's mind, it would take years and years of progress before ELIXIR achieved anything resembling true intelligence.

In the meantime, the lab presented conference papers at the IJCAI and the AAAI. They published scholarly articles in *Computing*. From time to time, an article appeared in a popular magazine like *Atlantic Monthly* or *Newsweek* about ELIXIR. David took no pleasure in this, avoiding the reporter, always sending another member of the lab to represent the group. He was famously camera-shy and would never let his picture be taken, even by Ada; the only recent image of her father that she had was one on an old photo ID that she had swiped from him when the system changed. In it, David looked at the camera askance, wincing, as if staring into a very bright light. With these publications, he cooperated only out of a sense of obligation to the Bit, because the publicity was helpful for generating funds. A laudatory article in *Time* was published in 1980, detailing the ambitions of the Steiner Lab; in the photograph, a smiling Hayato posed with his palm on the top of the monitor on which they chatted with ELIXIR: a proud father placing a protective hand on his child. David had refused the coverage, as usual, thrusting the other members of the lab forward, receding into the background himself.

Together, the members of the Steiner lab were generally reserved in their predictions about what ELIXIR could accomplish. They were self-disparaging and disparaging, too, of the program, whom they benevolently insulted, almost as sport. (Ada, who had grown fond of ELIXIR, was displeased by this; she felt it was somehow disloyal.)

But sometimes, when it was just Ada and David alone, he allowed himself to rhapsodize about the future of the beast, as he affectionately called ELIXIR from time to time, and he encouraged her to do so as well.

"What is the end result of a program like this one?" he asked Ada.

She studied his face, looking for hints.

"A companion?" she asked. "An assistant?"

"Possibly," said David, but he looked at her, always, as if waiting for more.

On Saturday, August 11, 1984, Ada woke up to find David missing. She knew he was gone as soon as she woke up: normally she could sense his presence in the house from the small noises he made, his constant movement, the vibration of the floor from a jittering leg. But that morning there was a foreign stillness to the house, a quietness that made her think, at first, that she was someplace else.

Despite this, her first notion was to look all over the house for him. Once, when she had thought he was out, she'd stumbled upon him in the basement, with industrial noise-canceling headphones on, working on an experiment that, he'd said, required his full concentration. But this time Ada did not find him.

There was no note. His car was still in the driveway. She searched for his keys and his wallet; the former she found, the latter she did not see. This meant, she presumed, that he had gone out on some errand, but had not intended to stay for long. He had left the kitchen door unlocked.

She told herself not to worry. David had, in recent months, been increasingly prone to disappearing without notice for brief periods of time. An hour or two or three would go by and then he would reappear from a walk, whistling cheerfully. When she asked after his whereabouts, he would answer vaguely about wanting fresh air. Once, she asked him to leave her a note when he was going out; though he agreed to, he had looked at her with an expression she interpreted as disappointment. That she was not more self-reliant; that she needed him in this way. Ada did not ask again. Instead, she attempted to train herself not to care.

Ada sat down at the kitchen table. She stood up, and then sat down again. She tried for a time to do the lesson he had most recently assigned her. It was a proof of Sierpinski's Composite Number Theorem, which normally would have interested her—but she could not concentrate. After another hour she called David's office at the lab. It was a Saturday, so she doubted any of his colleagues would be in. The phone rang six times and then came the click that meant the start of the answering machine—a device that David and Charles-Robert had invented and assembled at the lab one Sunday in the late 1970s, before they were widely available commercially. *This is Jeeves, the Steiner Lab's butler,* said the machine, which relied upon the earliest available text-to-speech software and therefore was barely comprehensible. *May I take your message?*

Ada hung up.

She checked the time: 11:44 a.m.

She negotiated with herself for a while about whether it was reasonable to call every hospital in Boston, and then decided that it would not be harmful, and that, besides, it would be something to do. It was possible, she thought, that he had gone out for a walk or a run and sustained some injury, major or minor, the latest in an impressive career of self-injury that, David had always told her, began when she was a child.

But nobody had any record of David Sibelius.

At 3:00 in the afternoon she began to have serious thoughts about calling the police, but she quickly decided against doing so. She had a feeling that he might somehow be in trouble if his own child reported him missing. David had always displayed, and had fostered in Ada, a low-level mistrust of the police, and of authority in general. One of his many obsessions was the importance of privacy; he often expressed a lack of faith in elected officials, a sort of mild skepticism of the government. Once, Ada had witnessed an accident in front of their house—nothing major, a minor scrape-up at most—and had asked David if they should call 911. At this he shook his head emphatically. "They'll be fine," he said, and added that he'd never known a more corrupt group of officials than the Boston Police Department, whom, if at all possible, the two of them should seek to avoid. In general, though, he came across merely as a far leftist with, perhaps, mild anarchist tendencies. In this way he was not so different from the rest of his colleagues.

She would call Liston, she decided.

Ada very rarely rang her at home. In general she did not like to use the telephone; she never seemed to know when to speak, and she did not know how to end conversations. She could hear her own breathing in the receiver as the phone rang once and then twice and then three times. She prayed that it would be Liston who answered the phone, but instead one of her three boys answered—Matty, Ada thought, because the voice was childish and high.

"Is Liston there?" she fairly whispered.

"Who is this?" asked Matty, and she told him it was Ada Sibelius.

"Mum," he called, without much urgency, "it's David's daughter." And finally Liston picked up the phone.

Ada didn't know what to say.

"Ada?" Liston asked. "Is everything all right?"

"Yes," said Ada.

"Are you just calling to say hi?" Liston asked her.

"No," said Ada.

"Well," said Liston. "What's going on?"

"When I woke up this morning David was gone," Ada said, "and he's still gone."

"Okay," said Liston. "He didn't leave a note?"

"No."

"Did you look all around the house?"

"Yes."

Liston said, "What time is it?" as if talking to herself, and then sighed.

Ada paused. She wasn't certain how to ask what she needed to ask. She wanted to know what Liston knew. "Do you know where he is?" she asked finally, because it was as close as she could come.

"I don't, honey," said Liston. "I'm sorry.

"Did you call the police?" asked Liston.

"No," said Ada, and then she said it again for emphasis.

Liston paused. "That might be a good thing to do," she said.

Ada was silent. She looked at the clock on the wall; watched its second-hand tick.

"I'm sorry, kiddo," said Liston finally. "Listen, come over. We can go for a drive and look for him, okay?"

Ada left a note for David before she left the house. It said, *David. I'm out looking for you with Liston. Please wait here until we're back. Ada.*

She put it on the kitchen table, facing the kitchen door, where he was most likely to see it upon his return. Though David and she always came through the side door of the house, nearest the kitchen, he insisted on letting visitors in through the front door. "It's nicer that way," he said once, when she asked why. He was like this, always: old-fashioned and formal in certain ways—he was knowledgeable, for example, on subjects such as tea and place settings, heraldry, forms of address—irreverent, outrageous, in others.

She walked outside toward Liston's house, and saw that Mrs. O'Keeffe, their next-door neighbor, was sitting in her lawn chair in her yard. She had macular degeneration and wore dark glasses all year-round. She was perhaps ninety years old, and in the warmer months she sat outside beginning at sunrise and only went in to eat. Ada walked over to her, and she raised a veined thin hand in greeting. Ada leaned down to address her.

"Mrs. O'Keeffe," Ada said to her, bent at the waist. "It's Ada Sibelius."

She turned her face up in Ada's direction. "Hello, Ada," she said.

"Did you see my father leave this morning, by any chance?" she asked.

"Let me think," said Mrs. O'Keeffe.

She put a hand to her cheek tremblingly.

"I believe I did," said Mrs. O'Keeffe.

"Was he carrying anything?" Ada asked.

"Now, I can't recall," said Mrs. O'Keeffe.

"Which way did he walk?"

"That way," she said, pointing down Shawmut Way toward Savin Hill Ave: the way one walked to cross over the bridge into the rest of Dorchester.

"What was he wearing?" Ada asked her. "Did he say hello to you?"

But again she couldn't recall.

Liston's car was a station wagon with wooden sides and a bench seat across the front. She was leaning against it when Ada arrived, and she held the passenger door open.

"Hi, baby," said Liston. She looked worried. She was wearing sunglasses on her head and an oversized windbreaker. They pulled out, and Liston turned left on Savin Hill Ave. She asked where Ada thought they should look for him and she suggested they go over the bridge, first to David's favorite restaurant, Tran's; and then to the library in Fields Corner; and then along Morrissey Boulevard, passing the beaches on the way to Castle Island, toward which David often jogged; and finally to the lab.

"Anyplace else?" asked Liston.

"I don't know," said Ada.

"He didn't give you any hints? He hasn't been talking about going anyplace in particular?"

"No," said Ada, wishing she could answer differently.

"And has he disappeared like this before?"

Ada hesitated. She did not want to tell Liston the truth, which was, of course, that he had. A few hours here, there. She settled on an answer that sounded all right in her head: "Just a couple of times," she said. "Never for long."

Liston shook her head. "Oh, David," she said, and in her voice Ada heard some piece of knowledge that she was not sharing.

It was true that Liston and David were close, and had been since he had hired her almost fifteen years before, but there was no one, Ada felt, who understood him as Ada herself did. She didn't like to hear Liston speak of him dismissively; she didn't want her to feel that they were conspiring, or that they shared any common criticisms of David.

Ada thought back to the telephone conversation she had overheard Liston having with David and wondered if there was any possible way to explain how she had come to overhear it. She decided, at last, that there was not. She wanted badly to know what Liston had been speaking of; not knowing made her feel less close to David. She had always imagined herself as his confidante, his right hand, and didn't like to think of anyone knowing something about him that she herself wasn't privy to.

"How long has he been gone now?" Liston asked, and Ada checked her watch. It was just after 3:00 in the afternoon.

"Eight hours," she said. "At least. I woke up at 7:00 and he was already gone."

"We'll give it a while longer," said Liston. "I called my friend Bobby in the police department, and he told me they wouldn't start searching until tomorrow anyway. Even if we called in." And she must have seen the nervous look on Ada's face, for she assured her that he would most likely be back before then.

"I bet you he'll be back by dinnertime," said Liston, but she, too, looked worried.

He had not been into Tran's, said Tran. "Is he okay?" he asked, and the two lines between his eyebrows deepened. He loved David.

Ada assured him that David was fine—digging down deep into her reserves of strength to do so—and then returned to Liston's car. They continued along for a time. Ada slumped against the seat, her head against the headrest, scanning the sidewalks on either side of the road for David. She searched the roadsides for his shining head, for a tall man in a T-shirt and shorts, or in trousers and a threadbare oxford, jangling his limbs about in a way that seemed incompatible with speed, and yet propelled him forcefully ahead.

Liston tried to make small talk with her, telling her one or another little anecdote about the grad students or about Martha, the division secretary—"All she wants, poor thing, is a date with a normal man"—but Ada could only muster the briefest of replies.

David was nowhere they looked.

Their drive became a silent one, strange and uncomfortable. For the first time, Ada allowed herself to truly wonder if her father was gone completely—disappeared altogether. Kidnapped. Dead on some lonesome road in the mountains of New Hampshire or New York. Or injured badly, unable to call for help. Or—worst of all—gone of his own volition. Was it possible, she wondered, that he had abandoned her? It was such a contrast to anything she understood about her father that she could not process the idea.

At last, they pulled back onto Shawmut Way, and Liston stopped in David's driveway, where his car was still parked. For several seconds neither of them moved. It was quiet: Ada could hear children playing a block away. Small clicks and pings emanated from beneath the hood of Liston's station wagon as the engine settled and cooled.

The house looked too still.

"I'll come in with you," said Liston, and together they exited the car and approached the house. Would her father be inside? Would he be frantic, apologetic? Would he have an explanation for them both?

Inside, it was quiet. "David?" called Ada, once, twice. But there was no response.

Liston turned to her. On her face Ada saw an expression that was meant to register as cheerfulness but came off as doubt.

Liston checked her watch, and Ada did the same: 5:00 in the evening.

"Tell you what," said Liston brightly. "Why don't you come over for a while? Pack some overnight things just in case. I'll go get a room ready back at the house."

Ada's heart increased its pace. The idea of spending time at Liston's, while her sons were there, was simultaneously appealing and terrifying.

"Come on," said Liston. "We'll get you a snack, too."

It was only then that Ada realized she had not eaten all day.

Upstairs, alone, Ada packed a nightgown, her hairbrush, some clothes for the next day (to pack more than these seemed pessimistic), and seven books, all into the little blue suitcase that was hers to use. David had a matching one in green. Then she went downstairs and wrote a new note for David.

David, it said. *I am really scared. Where are you? I'm at Liston's. Please call right away.*

And then, just in case, she wrote down Liston's number, too, which David knew like his own pulse.

She exited the kitchen, leaving the door unlocked for her father. She walked toward Liston's.

Liston's house had a front porch, and on it were two boys' bicycles leaned in toward one another, and a girl's pink bicycle with its tassels chopped off an inch from each handle. Someone had begun to color the pink seat black with a permanent marker, but had only gotten halfway. Like all the houses on the block, Liston's was a colorful Victorian, painted a different color every ten years or so. That decade it was light blue with dark blue shutters and edges. The porch itself had been painted the color of the trim, so that walking on it gave one the feeling of being underwater. It was nearly time for a new paint job; the existing color had begun to come up off the wooden floor and down from the ceiling, and small unsettled piles of paint chips had made their way into crevices and corners. Once or twice, Ada had seen Liston briskly sweeping the porch and the front walkway, but mainly she had no time for such details, preferring instead to maintain, she told Ada, the highest level of cleanliness her busy schedule would allow. She would not have dreamed of bringing in a cleaning service—to her they were for rich people.

Ada walked up the steps with great apprehension and raised her fist to knock softly on the door. No one answered. She looked at her watch and told herself that if, after two minutes, no one had answered, she would try again.

She did, with slightly greater force. And this time quick footsteps came rushing toward the door, and Matty opened it.

He said nothing. He was nine years old at the time, tall for his age. He had a feathery haircut, and he wore denim cutoffs and a red-striped tank top. Both knees were scraped up, and as he appraised Ada, he reached down to scratch at one of his scabs absentmindedly.

"Hi," Ada said.

"Hi."

"I'm here to see your mom," she told him. She felt ridiculous saying it: only four years older than he was, and yet playing the role of an adult, a friend of his mother's.

But at that moment Liston came into sight behind Matty, sock-footed.

"What are you doing, Matty? Open the door for Ada," she said, and then did it herself, and Matty shrugged and ran upstairs.

"No manners," said Liston, after Ada had stepped inside. Liston shut the inner door behind them. Liston hated the heat more than anyone Ada had ever met, and several years before had installed central air in her hundred-year-old house, which cost her more than she cared to admit. All spring Ada had seen men working on Liston's roof, coming and going through the front door. Now a large metal box occupied a space in her backyard, near the patio, and inside the house it felt calm and cool and shadowy. The sweat on Ada's neck cooled and disappeared.

She had only been in Liston's house a handful of times before. Normally when she and David got together outside work it was at a restaurant, or at David's house. In its layout her home was similar to David's—living room, sitting room, dining room, kitchen on the first floor; bedrooms above—but she had decorated it quite differently. All the upholstery was floral or patterned in some way, in accordance with the fashion of the decade. Large framed mirrors hung on some of the walls, so that Ada could not avoid seeing herself at every turn; prints of famous paintings or reproductions of movie posters hung on others.

Liston brought her into the kitchen, which was larger than David's, and sat Ada down at a built-in nook that looked something like a booth at a restaurant.

"What can I get you to eat, hon?" asked Liston, and rattled off a list of all the snacks of the 1980s that Ada was never permitted to have: canned pastas by Chef Boyardee, Fluffernutter sandwiches, fluorescent Kraft macaroni and cheese. In truth, Ada had never even heard of some of the food Liston offered her. She chose the sandwich, thinking it would mean the least work, and Liston scooped out something white and soft and put it on a piece of Wonder Bread, with peanut butter on another piece, and then she closed them together with a clap, and handed it to Ada with a glass of milk.

For a while she watched Ada eat. Then, finally, she spoke.

"What do you want to do? Do you want to watch TV?"

Ada opened and closed her mouth twice.

"Do you not watch TV?" Liston inquired.

"No, I do," said Ada, and told herself that it was not, in fact, a lie, because there was a police drama that David and she watched together sometimes, and occasionally David rented and watched old films or television shows on the VCR, which counted, she supposed.

Ada followed Liston into what she called "the TV room," which David would have called a sitting room, and there it was, a big box of a television, as big as any Ada had ever seen. Facing it was a couch with a right angle built into it. She sat down there, in the elbow of the curve. She put a pillow over her lap.

Liston turned on the television with a remote control, which she handed to Ada. "We just got cable," said Liston. "There are probably a hundred channels on there. I don't know what half of them are."

Ada inspected the remote. David had made a primitive variant that they used at home, but this one looked official, and had many more buttons.

"I'll be working in the kitchen if you need me," said Liston.

Ada flipped upward through the channels. The following images came onto the screen—and for the rest of her life, for reasons she could never explain, they stayed with her. A bride in a dress. Two men fishing. A gentleman walking through an empty home. Congresspeople debating. A redheaded girl with a redheaded boy. Somebody standing in a field of blue flowers. A cartoon of Superman flying. A movie about war, with soldiers climbing over a low stone wall. She left the last one on and watched as they advanced on the opposition. It looked like it was meant to be World War II, and the troops looked like they were meant to be British. David liked war movies. Ada knew about war.

She watched the entire film and then she began to watch the next one, which was its sequel, when suddenly she noticed someone standing next to her, in her peripheral vision. She kept her face turned very straight ahead, for she knew that it was one of Liston's older boys, and the possibility that it was William made her stiffen with nerves.

"What are you watching," said the boy. He had a low voice, much as she remembered William's voice sounding.

"I don't know," Ada whispered.

"You like this movie?" he asked.

"I don't think so," she whispered, but he must not have heard her, because he said, "You can't talk?"

Ada's voice had been taken from her, so she only shook her head. She could recall for the rest of her life the very particular feeling she had at that age, when asked to interact with a peer—it often seemed as if her voice had retreated into her stomach, which then clenched it very tightly and held it deeply inside of her, and wouldn't release it until she was alone once more.

Ada shifted her eyes as far to the left as they would go and made out a boy in a blue T-shirt with his hand on the back of the sofa. She let herself turn her head ever so slightly to more closely inspect his arm, which was sturdy and tan, and his hand at the end of it, which had nails that were very severely bitten, down to the part that hurts. She did not look up at his face.

Then he took his arm away and then he took himself away, out of the room. She breathed out heavily.

She was alone again.

At a certain point she could smell and hear Liston microwaving something, probably making dinner, and she knew then that it would be polite to go in and ask her if she needed help, but she was frightened of encountering any of the boys again, so she stayed where she was on the sofa. She was expecting a cry from Liston—*Dinner!* she might say, and the boys would come rushing to the kitchen—but it never came. Instead, Liston poked her head into the TV room and asked if she wanted to eat there or at the table.

"Either," Ada said, and Liston winked at her and said maybe the two of them should eat at the table, like civilized people. "David would be appalled if I let you watch too much TV."

Ada followed her into the kitchen and watched as, from the microwave, Liston pulled two frozen meals. *Dining-In,* said the packages on the counter. *Salisbury Steak Dinner.*

"Where are the boys?" Ada asked, before she thought better of it.

"Oh, they fend for themselves, mostly," said Liston lightly. "They don't like my cooking."

Ada was surprised. She had imagined, somehow, that everyone in this family ate together all the time. She had liked to imagine it that way.

They talked about anything but David: the latest gossip from the lab, the problem Liston was working on. At one point Matty came in and asked Liston if he could watch television, "now that she's not watching." And Liston told him all right, for fifteen minutes, but then he had to get ready for bed.

Soon there was a knock at the door. Her heart surged: it was David, she thought, at last. But Liston looked as if she had been expecting one.

"WILLIAM," she called loudly, without turning around.

Her oldest son came running down the stairs and around the corner, into the kitchen, and Ada, for the first time, allowed herself to look fully at his face, which was more handsome than she had remembered it. She looked away again quickly. He opened the door and said nothing. A girl his age came in and shut the door behind her. She was tall and skinny, with blond hair and an arc of sideways bangs, and she wore a shirt that hung off her shoulder, a bra strap showing itself assertively. She wore high heels, too. Ada thought she was pretty, but not quite as good-looking as William.

"Hey, Miz Liston," said the girl, and Liston said, "Hello, Karen," but didn't look up. William and Karen went upstairs together.

"That door better be open when I come upstairs," Liston called after them.

When Ada finished her dinner she was not sure where to go. So she very quietly picked up her fork and rinsed it at the sink, and then opened the dishwasher, but she wasn't certain whether to put it on the top or the bottom. David and she did not have a dishwasher.

"Just leave it in the sink, honey," said Liston.

When Ada turned around, Liston was looking at her, arms crossed. She glanced at the clock on the wall and back again. It was 9:00 at night.

"Should we try David one more time?" asked Liston, and Ada said yes, gratefully. She had not wanted to be the one to ask. But when she called her home number, no one was there.

"I think I'll go to bed now," said Ada. She was not tired, but it seemed the most out-of-the-way thing to do.

"Okay," said Liston. She put her hands on her hips for a moment and regarded her.

"We're glad you're here," she said, and it made Ada buckle for reasons she couldn't explain.

"C'mere," said Liston. She brought Ada to her, and kept her in her arms. Ada had rarely, in her life, been hugged, and she stiffened.

"It'll be all right," said Liston. "You'll be just fine." She did not, however, say that David would return.

The bedroom Liston put Ada in was decorated in shades of red and blue and green. It contained a small Lego-land that someone had labored over in the corner, and a twin bed with a frame shaped like a racecar.

"This is Matty's room," said Liston, "but I've thrown him in with Gregory for the night."

Ada did not like the idea of Matty's being thrown anywhere because of her, but Liston assured her that he would like it. "He'll get a kick out of it," she said. "He's obsessed with his older brothers."

"Can I get you anything else?" Liston asked. "A glass of water? The bathroom's down the hall."

Ada said that she was fine, and Liston put one hand on her head and looked at her, and told her again that it would be all right. Then she left her alone in Matty's room.

Liston's house was built so much like David's that Ada knew where she was going without asking. She got out her toothbrush and changed into her nightgown. She walked toward the bathroom at one end of the dim upstairs hallway and she passed an open door on her way there. She looked into the room as she did, and inside of it she saw William and Karen kissing on the bed. For one moment, she froze—trying to decide, perhaps, whether to retreat to her room or advance to the bathroom—and she stared. She had never seen a real-life kiss before, and the heads of the parties involved moved about in a surprisingly vigorous way. In the movies Ada had seen, old-fashioned ones that David and she watched together, the heads of the protagonists stayed coolly in place at an elegant angle as they embraced.

Suddenly William looked up and saw her. "*What* the *hell*," he shouted. He stood up and slammed the door.

"Oh my God, Will," she heard Karen say.

"She came out of nowhere," she heard William say.

Ada burned with embarrassment. She looked down at her plaid nightgown. It had ruffled wrists and a ruffled hem and was befitting of a much younger child or an old lady. She stood in place and thought about what she had done for a time, and then, afraid that William would fling open the door again, she continued to the bathroom, where she brushed her teeth with her finger and with toothpaste she borrowed from the Listons, having forgotten her own, and then she took her glasses off and splashed cold water on her face and patted it dry with someone else's towel, which smelled like cologne and was stiffer than it should have been.

After that she walked quickly back to her room, looking straight ahead in case William's door was open again, and closed the door behind her.

She stood in place for a while, breathing. She was not tired yet, and everyone else was still awake. She stayed up late into the night in Matty's room, reading one of the seven books that she had brought along with her, and eventually succumbing to the temptation of the hundreds of Legos in a bucket in the corner—they had been her favorite when she was younger, and a favorite of David's, too—and assembling a little castle with a drawbridge, a king, and a princess.

When, finally, she went to bed, it was difficult to fall asleep. She missed their house and she missed David.

To comfort herself, she imagined the worlds that were orbiting inside of every closed door along the hallway: Matty and Gregory in Gregory's room, breathing slowly in and out as they drifted toward sleep; and William and Karen kissing violently on William's bed; and the sheets and towels resting in the linen closet; and the spiders in the basement, spinning their webs, and every small living thing in the house—the dust mites, the gnats; and the water dripping out of the bathroom sink; and below her, Liston, old friend, scratching away at her yellow pad on work for the Steiner Lab, which was their second home.

And she wondered about David, where he might be.

In her mind, she went through the steps of their after-dinner ritual, which began while Ada cleaned up the dishes. Next she would go and stand outside David's office. His door was always open but a sort of impenetrable field surrounded him if he was working. Since the time she was small she had known the importance of never interrupting him. So she would press her head into the doorframe and stand on the edges of her sneakers and wait, and wait. And then, finally, he would turn to her and smile, as if waking from a dream.

"Let me explain something to you," he would say.

And then they would sit together at the dining room table and start on a lesson, one of the many thousands that he taught her in her life.

When she asked him a question that he thought was intelligent he slapped one hand down on the table in celebration. "That is exactly the question to ask," he told her.

When she asked him a question that revealed some chasm in her learning, some gap where a concept should have existed, he put his head in his hands as if trying to summon the energy to explain all that would need to be explained to her to make her fully formed. But he didn't despair: he started from a point that was more rudimentary than he thought necessary (generally it was, in fact, necessary) and proceeded from there, his graceful geometrical hands drawing diagrams on the pads of paper that he collected from conferences and hotels and then hoarded in his desk. He often said he could not speak without a pen in his hand. He waved with his pen, pointed with it, scribbled absentmindedly when on a telephone call. He drew funny things like flowers and birds when he was talking to Ada, and sometimes during her lessons. For the rest of her life, Ada did this, too. She adopted many of David's habits. They were alike: everyone said it. And that he understood her—more than anyone else in the world ever understood her—seemed to her like an incredible stroke of luck. "You are more machine than human, Ada," he said at times. And it was the truth, not an insult. And it was calming to her to be so understood. And, sometimes, she felt it was why he loved her.

She thought of this image as she tried to fall asleep. She pictured herself with David at his desk, the two of them bowing their heads together, their minds a Venn diagram—Ada's mind full of childish trivia, and David's full of the mysteries of the universe, and the center between them growing, growing. In these moments he was Zeus to her, and she Athena, springing fully formed from the head of her father, alight with grace and wisdom. There they were at the lab or at home, the two of them, always the two. There they were solving whatever problem it was that she was facing.

In the morning, Ada was woken from a dream about David by the sound of the bedroom door creaking slowly open. There in the doorway stood Matty, holding a canvas tote bag and observing her. She sat up in bed and rubbed her hands over her face.

"I just have to get some stuff out of here," said Matty, and then he came in and gathered up all of his Lego people and parts, two books, a small portable radio with a trailing wire. All of this he stuffed into his canvas bag, looking sideways at her as he did.

He sidled toward her before he left the room. He said to Ada, "Where's your dad?"

She lifted her shoulders and lowered them slowly. She kept her face very still.

Then he turned on his heel and closed the door firmly behind him. Ada heard him running down first one and then another flight of stairs, into the basement, she assumed.

Ada rose and tiptoed to the door and put her head out into the hallway. It was a Sunday, and everyone else seemed to be asleep still. As quietly as she could, she descended the stairs and went into the kitchen, where Liston's work was sprawled out over the table, and a yellow phone was mounted to the wall. She lifted the receiver from its cradle and dialed the number for her and David's house, holding her breath while the rings came, four in a row, five, ten. Nobody answered.

Then, hanging up the telephone, she pondered her options. It still felt odd to be in Liston's house for almost the first time after so many years of knowing her. She had no idea about Liston's habits or her daily routines—no idea, for example, whether she was an early riser on weekends or preferred to sleep late, and no idea what she did when she was not at work and not with David. If Ada had been at home with David, she would have known what to expect from her weekend: David would have stayed in his home office for most of the day, breaking for every meal; Ada would have read or worked on the assignments that David gave her. Some weekends they did something different and interesting: a trip to a nearby mountain for skiing in the winter, for example; or, in the summer, a trip to a cabin in upstate New York that David had been renting since the fifties; or some other excursion to a nearby town or city. Sometimes they went to Washington, D.C.; David had a friend there named George, an artist, one of the few people he had kept in touch with from his childhood. He also went on several work trips a year, to conferences in locations as mundane as Cleveland and as far-flung as Hong Kong. These counted as their vacations: typically they would stay a few extra days in every place, seeing more than they otherwise would have. Sometimes, if he'd be in meetings all day and he thought that Ada would have nothing to do, he went by himself to conferences; on these occasions, he paid the division secretary, Martha, to stay with Ada at the house on Shawmut Way, and returned as quickly as he could. And there were, of course, the yearly trips to New York City, always in winter, always to see the Christmas concert at Calvary Episcopal. On those same trips, they would see an opera or a ballet at Lincoln Center, and visit the Met, and walk in Central Park. David always reserved the same accommodations: two adjacent rooms on the third floor of a bed-and-breakfast in Brooklyn Heights ("Manhattan is overpriced," he always said, though Ada secretly wondered if he wished to limit, as much as possible, his chances of running into acquaintances from his past), owned by a charming, fragile septuagenarian named Nan Rockwell. She served scones for breakfast and talked with David about classical music until late into the night, playing on her turntable famous recordings that she sought out and traded for like cards. Always, they had dinner at a little cafeteria near Union Square, a nondescript place that David said reminded him of his youth, for reasons he did not explain to Ada.

Ada did not think Liston had any interest in doing these things. She came on most of the work-related trips that Ada and David took, but kept to herself, proclaiming her hatred for hotel rooms and her love of home. In her tastes she was polite but not adventuresome; she hopefully scanned every English-language menu they were presented for its blandest, palest dish. Until yesterday, Ada had always imagined that she did cozy things on weekends, made popcorn, watched movies with her boys, cooked meals with her oldest, Joanie, when she stopped by with the baby. How Ada came up with this idea, she was not certain: she had no reason to believe that the scientifically inclined Liston was domestic in any way. She knew that Liston did not like to cook, and could not abide housework. (She bragged often about raising her boys to be good husbands, assigning the weekly chores on a magnetic whiteboard that she stuck to the refrigerator.) Despite this, she still seemed *traditional* to Ada, in a way that Ada and David were not, and in a way—if she was honest with herself—that she envied. Liston drank Diet Coke. She brought ham-and-cheese sandwiches to work, on white bread. The sight of them made Ada's mouth water. The idea of Liston's house as a bastion of normalcy and tradition, right down the street, was one that Ada had always kept dear: it seemed somehow to anchor her and

David's house physically, in the same way that Liston's friendship with them proved reassuringly to Ada that there was nothing so unusual about her situation, after all.

It was not until shortly after nine that Ada noticed any movement upstairs. Upon hearing it, she tiptoed to the downstairs bathroom to hide, in case it was one of the boys. She did not want to greet them before their mother was there to protect her.

Ada heard footsteps walking down the stairs and into the kitchen, just as she had done, and then someone picked up the telephone receiver. She could hear it all quite clearly.

"It's Di," said Liston, in the other room.

Ada didn't know whom she had called, but she began to describe to the person the events of the day and night before, beginning with Ada's phone call to her. Ada froze. She thought perhaps she should clear her throat or turn on the water to let Liston know she was there, but she was immobilized by shyness and fear. She stood still, clutching herself around the middle.

"She's still at my house. She's upstairs sleeping," said Liston.

She paused.

"And what if he's not back today? When do we call the police?" said Liston.

And then, "He might get in trouble. It might affect Ada. What if they say he's incompetent?

"It's a sin," said Liston. "An honest sin."

After Liston hung up she began to move around the kitchen, opening cabinets. Ada held her breath. She didn't think she could emerge, just yet—Liston would know she had heard everything. She decided to wait until Liston went upstairs again, or into a different room, at which point she could make a quick exit and pretend she had been someplace else.

Ada sat down on the closed lid of the toilet. *Incompetent,* Liston had said. It was the word she had used about David. It contrasted with every understanding of her father that Ada had. She put her face into her hands. And at that moment Liston opened the bathroom door, and shouted in surprise.

She clutched her heart and doubled over. "Ada!" she said. "What on earth."

"I'm really sorry," said Ada, not knowing what else to say.

"Are you all right?" Liston asked her, and she nodded.

Liston put her hand to her chin, as if in thought. She was wearing a blue terry robe that looked perhaps a decade old.

"Did you hear me talking on the phone?" she asked Ada, and Ada had the urge to lie, but could not do it. Liston would have known. She nodded once more.

Liston took in a deep breath and exhaled slowly. "I'm sorry, baby," she said. She opened and closed her mouth, as if deciding whether to say more, and then gestured with her head that Ada should follow her into the kitchen, which she did.

"How'd you sleep?" she asked, and Ada said that the bed was very comfortable, and that she had slept excellently, though it wasn't true.

"Are you hungry?" Liston asked, and she nodded. On the kitchen counter was a line of boxed cereals, with a gallon of whole milk at the end. "Bowls there, spoons there," Liston said, pointing.

What David called cereal was hot and eaten with brown sugar. Ada had never before had cold cereal, and she inspected her options carefully, searching for the one that David would be least likely to bring into the house. At last she chose one called Smacks because of the happy frog on the box, one arm extended skyward, proudly presenting its bounty.

While she ate she waited for Liston to speak. She had settled down at the kitchen table, where her papers were still spread out from the night before, and was working out some problem with her pen, as if solving it would help her answer the larger question facing them. Handwritten code blossomed across the page. At that moment a great longing came over Ada for David and for their home. Every so often

Liston looked up at her and smiled, but she did not speak: as if waiting for Ada to confess something, some information she had previously kept to herself. But Ada had none.

"Are you going to church today?" Ada asked. She knew that Liston was an active member of the parish just over the bridge, and often on Sundays she had seen Liston marching there and back again with her boys, who were always dressed in ill-fitting khakis, button-down shirts, loose ties, scuffed and poorly knotted shoes. It occurred to her that day that Liston was not dressed for it; she did not wish to be the cause of any change in plans.

"We'll skip it today," said Liston, smiling. "The boys will be thrilled."

She put her pen down then and looked out the window. She spoke without shifting her gaze.

"What have you noticed, Ada?" she said.

"What do you mean?" Ada asked. She hated this: the feeling of being asked to betray David.

"About your dad," said Liston. "Has he been acting differently? Has he said anything strange?"

"I think he's just under a lot of stress," Ada said, and Liston nodded noncommittally.

Both of them were silent, and then both spoke at the same time. Ada said, "I think he'll be all right." And Liston said, "Honey. I think we should call the police."

Ada thought of David's mistrust of law enforcement; his vehement disapproval of the meddlesome State; his passionate dedication to privacy. And then she decided that whatever fear he had of the police, hers was greater of losing him.

"All right," she said, and immediately felt unfathomably disloyal, treacherous. She lowered her head.

Ada disliked the two police officers who arrived later that afternoon. She couldn't help it; her well had been poisoned by David's mistrust of authority. One was tall and thin; the other short and thin. Both had mustaches.

"And the last time you saw him was?" asked the tall one, Officer Gagnon.

"And has he been acting unusual?" he asked.

"And do you have any idea where he might be?" he asked.

He seemed bored. Both accepted Liston's offer of coffee, and then sipped it loudly.

"You're the daughter?" asked the shorter one, finally, and Ada said yes. "And how do you two know each other?" he asked, gesturing back and forth between Liston and her with his pen.

Liston explained, and the two of them looked at each other.

"We'll have to get social services in here," said Officer Gagnon. "Since there's no relation."

"Really? Are you sure?" said Liston. "I've known her since she was born."

"Sorry, ma'am," said Gagnon. "Just procedure. They'll be over soon."

It was then, for the first time, that Ada let her imagination run its terrifying course. She was an impressionable child, and she thought of what ruins might await her: she had read too much Dickens. Did workhouses still exist?

Before they left, Matty came into the kitchen—the suddenness and quietness of his appearance gave Ada the impression that he had been eavesdropping on them from someplace nearby—and looked shyly at the officers.

"Hey, big guy," said Gagnon, on his way out.

"Hey," said Matty, softly, but the door was already closed.

There was little to say for quite some time. Ada sat still at the kitchen table, pretending to read a newspaper, until at last Liston said that it must be close to dinnertime, and stood up, and went to the cupboards. She opened them one at a time, looked inside them beseechingly. At last she pulled down a blue box of spaghetti and some canned tomato sauce and opened both, started a pot of water.

"Are you all right?" Liston asked Ada at one point, and Ada nodded. But the truth was, of course, that she was not—would not be until David had returned. If he returns at all, she thought, and put her chin in her hands to keep it from trembling.

She stood up from the table abruptly. She had never cried in front of Liston before, and she didn't wish to now.

"I think I should get a few more clothes from my house," said Ada, and walked quickly out the door before Liston could follow her, or agree.

She inhaled deeply, willing herself to calm down. Outside it was beautiful. It had cooled off slightly for the first time that August. In the distance the low hum of a lawn mower started. One of the neighbors was barbecuing. The smell of burning charcoal and meat, the particulates of matter that found their way to her on a pleasant breeze, normally signaled happiness and relaxation to Ada. Ever since learning about neurotransmitters from David, she had imagined her brain as a water park, a maze of waterslides down which various chemicals were released. Charcoal and smoke and fresh-cut grass usually sent rivers of serotonin down the slides in Ada's head, as she pictured them. But that night the scents only served to remind her of David's absence. Warm summer evenings, he always said, were his favorites, too.

Ada let herself in through the kitchen door and poured a glass of water from the tap. She took it with her to her room at the top of the stairs and gazed out the window, and then felt drawn to the old computer at her little desk. She turned it on. She dialed into the ELIXIR program. She began to type. There was something comforting in the familiarity of ELIXIR's responses, the small turns of phrase she recognized as having come from colleagues at the lab. *Where is David?* she typed, and ELIXIR said, *That's really a very good question.* An answer that reminded her, in fact, of David's syntax.

There was a great deal to tell ELIXIR. It had only been two days since their last conversation, but it felt like it had been much longer. She looked at the clock after twenty minutes and, fearing that Liston would worry, shut down the program and then the computer, which gave a long sweet sigh as it went to sleep.

It was then that she thought she heard someone moving downstairs. She held her breath, listened for several more seconds.

A drawer opened someplace deep in the house. The basement, she thought. Footsteps. Someone dropped something on the floor. Someone began to walk up the basement stairs.

Ada was easily frightened as a child and she sat frozen in place, clutching her water glass, terrified to move. She eyed the window, measuring whether she could jump out of it if necessary. She decided, at last, that the thing to do was to ascertain the identity of the other person in the house as quickly as possible, so that—if necessary—she could make her escape.

"David?" she called out, loudly, bravely.

There was no answer. She tensed, prepared to run.

"David?" she called again.

"Hello," said David, his voice warm and familiar. "Is that you, Ada?"

She went limp. All of her muscles contracted and then relaxed. She had not realized the weight of the fear she had been holding in her gut, the tension of it; she felt as if she were breathing out completely for the first time in her life. Her face was crumpled and red when she descended the stairs and met her father in the kitchen. He paused with a hand on the wall. He was holding a notepad in his other hand and he had one of his contraptions, which looked something like ski goggles, pushed back on his head.

"Good grief," said David. "What's the matter, Ada?" The look he wore was a sort of perplexed smile, as if they were about to discover a grand misunderstanding that they would look back on one day and find comical.

"Where have you *been*," she lamented. "Where did you go?"

Her voice must have conveyed a very particular emotion—it was anger at David's betrayal of her trust. From the time she was small, she had felt it whenever she was embarrassed in public, with him by her side: while skiing, for example, if she fell down and, in the tangle of her equipment, could not immediately get up. "*Help* me," she would mutter to David, under her breath. She always sensed, somehow, that it was his fault she had fallen down. She felt the weight of others' stares upon her, seethed in her own embarrassment, converted it into anger at her father. He seemed so well equipped to deal with anything, so utterly competent: and this made her feel that it was his responsibility to preempt and prevent any mistake, any humiliation, not just for himself but for her. Standing in the kitchen, staring at her prodigal father, she felt the same emotion, only stronger: thinking of what she would have to tell Liston, what Liston would invariably tell her boys. In that moment, Ada knew for the first time she could no longer hope to protect David from Liston's judgment, from anyone's judgment—as she had been doing, if she was honest with herself, for over a year.

David had not answered her yet. He was looking at her in a hazy, puzzled way.

"David," she said again.

"I told you," he said finally, speaking carefully, measuring his words. "I told you I was going out of town for work."

As an adult, when Ada tried to recall her father's face, it was often and regrettably this version of him that she thought of: David looking mad, ski goggles pushed back on his head, his shirtsleeves rolled up. There was little connection to David as he normally was, placid, reserved, attentive. This David was growing increasingly stubborn with every additional question he was asked. He had been in New York City, he said, meeting with the chair of the Computer Science Department at NYU. Ada tried to convince him to come back with her to Liston's, but he wouldn't.

She studied him for a moment.

"Really, this is silly, Ada," he told her. "A simple misunderstanding. I'm in the middle of an experiment." He held forth the notepad he was carrying as if by way of explanation. Pointed to the device on his head.

"Wait right here, then," said Ada, and she ran to get Liston.

Inside Liston's house, Liston was pouring the pasta into a colander in the sink. Steam rose up from the boiling water and wilted her hair.

"He's back," Ada told her. "He says he was out of town for work. He says he told me. Maybe I forgot."

It pained her to say it.

Liston looked at Ada uncomprehendingly for a moment and then followed her out the door, down the street to her house. By the time they reached David, he was back in the basement, bent over the device he had been wearing, turning into place a tiny screw.

"Shhhhhhhh," he said, as Liston began to speak.

"Honestly, David," said Liston. "Enough of this."

He straightened and then looked wounded.

"You've been gone for almost forty-eight hours," said Liston. "Where were you?"

"I was in New York for work," he said slowly. "For heaven's sake. I wasn't gone long at all." But his face was changing.

"What work?" she asked him.

He looked down at the workbench. Spun the device on the table in a full circle.

Liston folded her arms.

"It's time to tell Ada," said Liston. "David? Do you hear me?"

They brought Ada to the living room to deliver the news. Later, she recalled wondering, perversely, if this was what it was like to have both a father and a mother. They sat together across from her. She was on a little chair that David said had come from his grandmother. They were on a leather sofa that David attended to from time to time with an oil that smelled like lemons.

David looked at Liston for help, but she shook her head.

He cleared his throat.

"Two years ago," he began, "at Liston's insistence, I visited a doctor for the first time in quite a while. There I was instructed to return for further testing. Upon doing so, I was informed that it was likely that I might be in the early stages of Alzheimer's disease. I disagreed with that assessment. I still do."

He paused.

"How familiar are you with Alzheimer's disease?" he asked.

Ada considered, and then said she knew what it was. She had read about it in some book or other, or perhaps more than one book. It was part of her vocabulary. She pictured it as a slow gray fog that rolled in over one's memory. She pictured it seeping in through the doors and windows as they spoke, invading the room. She felt cold.

"Have you been back to the doctor since then?" Ada asked.

Liston glared at David.

"No," he said, hesitantly.

"What?" he said to Liston. "There's nothing they can do for me. Even if their diagnosis is correct."

"You seem fine," Ada said to him, and to Liston, and to herself.

"I am," he said. "Don't worry too much about this, Ada," he said. "I'm quite all right."

Ada could feel the tension between David and Liston. She knew, though she was young, what was causing it: it was Liston's wish to protect her with honesty, and David's to protect her—and himself—with optimism, wishfulness, some willful ignorance of his impending fate.

"I think David might have told me he'd be going out of town, actually," said Ada. "I can't remember now."

It was a lie. Of course it was a lie. Liston looked at her sadly.

"You see?" said David, but Liston didn't respond.

Finally, in the midst of their silence, Ada stood up. She turned to Liston.

"I guess I can stay here now," she said, and she excused herself, and walked slowly up the stairs to her bedroom, which was as unfrilled and austere as a man's, wallpapered in a brown plaid that the previous owners had chosen. She'd been reading *The Way of a Pilgrim*, like Franny Glass, and although she was not religious, she said the Jesus Prayer aloud, quietly, five times. She told herself that everything would be fine, because she could imagine no alternative. Because no life existed for her outside of David.

In a week, the Boston Department of Children & Families came to visit them. Liston had called Officer Gagnon to let him know that

David had been found, but they were concerned enough about his disappearance to investigate.

David was appalled. He sulked his way through the home visit, with a woman named Regina O'Brien, a gray lady with gray hair. To her questions he gave single-word answers, sometimes unsubtly rolling his eyes. In order to offer an explanation for an absence that had brought the police to their home, David was forced to reveal his diagnosis to the DCF. His first proposal that he had simply forgotten to tell Ada that he'd been going out of town had seemed to alarm them more than it assured them of his competence.

Then came a question that David and Ada had not prepared for in advance. Miss O'Brien looked at Ada and asked how she was doing in school.

Ada paused. She looked at David, who looked at Miss O'Brien and told her that Ada was doing very well in school.

It was not, perhaps, a lie, if one counted David's method of educating her at his laboratory as *school.* He had always been hazy about homeschooling Ada; in that decade, everyone thought it was odd and eccentric, but not out of line with the rest of David's odd, eccentric behavior. Everyone, including Ada, seemed to accept that he had worked something out with the state. In that moment, for the first time, it occurred to Ada that perhaps he never had.

It must have occurred to Regina O'Brien, too, for she looked at Ada levelly and asked her what school she attended.

She panicked. She looked at David, who said nothing. She thought she should lie. "Woodrow Wilson," she said, naming a nearby middle school, uncertain whether it was even the one she'd be sent to.

"And what grade are you in?" asked Miss O'Brien.

"Eighth," said Ada.

Miss O'Brien paused.

"And who's your favorite teacher there?" she asked.

At last, David interjected. "She doesn't go anyplace. I teach her," he said. "I provide an education for her at home and at my place of work."

And from the look on Miss O'Brien's face, Ada knew that they were deeply in trouble.

Later in the 1980s, a series of cases worked their way through the Massachusetts courts that would define the laws that now govern the idea of homeschooling. In *Care and Protection of Charles & Others*, one will find an overview of what is now required of homeschoolers in the state of Massachusetts: Prior approval from the superintendent and school board, for one. Access to textbooks and resources that public school children use, for another. David and Ada had neither. In 1984, David's failure to enroll his daughter in any school was only further evidence of his neglect, in the eyes of the DCF.

He seemed not to recognize the severity of the allegations against him. He felt it was impossible that they could take his child from him. Absurd. He told Liston it would not happen.

But after that first visit, their lives began to change. The DCF commanded David to enroll Ada in an accredited school. Miss O'Brien recommended to her supervisor that home visits be continued, and social services required David to see a doctor regularly to monitor the progress of his disease. To see whether, and how fast, he was progressing toward parental incompetence. Incompetence: the word that Liston had once used in reference to him. Incompetence: the opposite, to Ada, of her father's name.

The Queen of Angels School was a brown brick building, four stories high, set close to the sidewalk. One wide short flight of stairs led to six unpretty industrial doors, painted a dull dark blue. Its roof, surrounded by high chain-link fences on all sides, was used for gym class in warm weather. Its lower windows had metal bars running from top to bottom—added several decades after the school was first built, an attempt to calm paranoid parents who increasingly saw Dorchester as a place to be feared—and its upper windows were narrower and more numerous than what would have been standard for the building, which gave it the look of a medieval fortress or a city wall.

On a Wednesday in September, more than a week after the school year had begun for everyone else, Ada walked for the first time into the Queen of Angels Lower School. Liston and David were with her; all three had taken the day off of work. For the weeks following the DCF's visit, there had been a debate. David had wanted to enroll her in the local public junior high, but Liston had insisted that that would not do. So, grumblingly, David and Ada and Liston had gone at the start of the month to meet with Sister Aloysius, the principal, and Mr. Hanover, the president, both of whom were in charge of welcoming new students into their fold.

In the high-ceilinged office occupied by the latter, the three of them sat and listened to a speech about the benefits of a Catholic education, the moral enlightenment Ada would receive, the community provided by the school. David leaned forward in his chair, his elbows on his knees, looking down at the floor, the top of his bald head catching light from the window and shining. He sat up, stretched his arms and legs uncomfortably, sighed out heavily once or twice. Liston glared at him. Ada hoped that no one else noticed.

The two administrators were tactful about her history, referring to her homeschooling only vaguely, euphemistically, as if it might behoove everyone to forget about it entirely. Ada assumed that Liston, who was well known in the Queen of Angels parish and active in the school, had prepped them thoroughly.

Ada listened attentively to everything that was said, looking around with interest at the decorations and the architecture: the crucifixes on the walls, above all the doors; the ancient, ticking clocks in metal cages; the colors of the school, which had most likely been redone in the previous decade and consisted mainly of muted, modernist tones. Pea-green, goldenrod, maroon. She felt in certain ways that she had breached a castle wall; she had so often walked past Queen of Angels and scanned its exterior for signs of what it must be like inside. As outsiders, David and Ada had always been only hazily aware of the ways in which Dorchester was divided, though it interested David, and he often asked Liston to describe it. To Liston, to her children and friends, one's parish was more important than one's neighborhood or one's street. The first floor of Queen of Angels contained the local parish school, a grammar school, perhaps two hundred students in sum from kindergarten through eighth grade. But the upper floors contained a central diocesan high school that drew from seven different parochial schools, including the one beneath it, and so beginning in the ninth grade the school widened into a river of students from a broader swath of Dorchester, and some from the city beyond. Nearly everyone in Savin Hill, including all three Liston boys, attended

Queen of Angels: Matty and Gregory in the Lower School, William in the Upper. Liston herself had gone there for her entire education as a girl. This was the only fact about the school that David found at all reassuring. "Well, I suppose it did all right by Liston," he said to Ada, but a note of skepticism still made its way into his voice. Ada would enter as an eighth-grader, based on her age and not much else, and be placed among students who had known each other for years. But Sister Aloysius assured her that by ninth grade she would blend right in.

At one point, she leaned in toward Ada kindly and put a hand on the desk. "Ada, dear," she said, "if ever you find yourself unable to grasp something, or falling behind in a course, don't hesitate to come to me for help."

At this David's head jerked to attention and, finally, he spoke. "There is no question that Ada will be able to *grasp* what you put before her," he said, a sort of quiet viciousness making its way into his voice. "In fact, I'd go so far as to say she'll throttle it. The question is whether you'll be able to provide my daughter with the sort of material that will offer her even the slightest challenge. Or do you," he said. "Or do you," he said again, and then he lost his words.

All of them, including David, fell for a moment into silence.

"I can guarantee you, sir," began Mr. Hanover, at the same time that Liston stood up and thanked them for their time.

"Do you have any questions?" asked Sister Aloysius, looking only at Ada, and Ada shook her head quickly in response.

Later that day, Liston called to ask whether Ada would like her boys to walk her to school in the morning. She declined, not wanting to saddle them with her, feeling sure that the request would be a burden to them. The recent turmoil in her life had momentarily supplanted her crush on William as the place her thoughts wandered when left undirected. She realized that she had not daydreamed about him for a week.

In the evening, David mustered up some energy and made them both dinner. "Whatever you like, Ada," he said. She had chosen *pot au feu*, a special favorite of hers that David made only on occasion, and went with him to the butcher on Dot Ave to pick up the beef.

She let him amble ahead of her and concentrated on his walk, memorizing it, wondering what it would be like to be without him. For the past several weeks she had been investigating Alzheimer's disease on her own, with the help of the scholarly library at the Bit. She had discovered two things: first, that the disease typically moved at a fairly sedate pace. Life expectancy, in that decade, was thought to be about eight to ten years from diagnosis. But it had been over two years already since he was first forced by Liston to see a doctor, and—if Ada was honest with herself—she had been noticing symptoms of forgetfulness for longer than that. She had been convincing herself for years that David had always been absentminded.

The second bit of information that she learned, more troublingly, was that when the disease was diagnosed in younger people, its progression was often more rapid. David was fifty-nine: well below the age the literature listed as the cutoff point between early-onset Alzheimer's and the more typical variety. And in early-onset patients, the disease could move quite fast: two or three years until the individual's comprehension skills were entirely lost, until the individual was no longer verbal. After that, quite rapidly, the function of his muscles and all of his reflexes would shut down completely.

Ada had squeezed her eyes shut against this possibility. She told herself it would not happen: that David would be the exception.

The butcher shop was busy with customers, but the owner knew and loved her father.

"What can I get you, Professor?" he asked—his perpetual name for David, and for anyone in the neighborhood who manifested signs of formal education—and David, leaning forward, his hands behind his back, selected his cut of beef carefully, brought it home, cooked it up for Ada while she sat in the kitchen and talked to him, her father, her best and most important ally in the world.

"I'll tell you something, Ada," said David. He turned to look at her, pushed his glasses, steamy from the pot of water he had boiling on the stove, back up on his nose. "It's going to be a different lab without you there. Quite a different lab altogether," he said. "I know Liston's really going to miss you."

"I'll miss her, too," said Ada. She was talking, of course, about her father; just as he was talking about her.

Their old and comfortable house filled up with the smell of herbs and onions and garlic. And Ada thought in that moment that it might not all be so bad.

Liston had warned her not to be late, so before she went to bed Ada had consulted the schedule she'd received, noting the start time of all the classes. Her first was at 8:00 a.m., and she planned on arriving at 7:50 just to be safe.

At breakfast, David was quiet. He did not know what to say to her: she could tell that he felt he had failed her.

Then he asked, as if it had just occurred to him, what she would use to carry her books, and she pointed to a canvas bag on the floor that she had scavenged from the basement.

"Oh, dear," said David. "That won't do the trick. Wait here," he said, and he went into his office and emerged, proudly, with a brown briefcase that unlocked only when a five-digit code was entered mechanically onto a rotating combination lock. David had not used it in years, but it had been an object of fascination for Ada when she was small. He had programmed the lock with a number he promised she could guess. As a smaller child she had spent hours entering guess-able numbers: her birth date, then her birth date backward; his birth date, forward and backward; the address of their house with three zeroes in front of it. But she'd never guessed correctly. Every now and then, still, she walked into his office and idly tried a new idea.

"It's yours," he said to her proudly.

She took it from him. She was pleased: she felt professional, suddenly, like her own person.

"You've never guessed the code?" he asked.

Ada shook her head.

"It's just *code*. The word *code*, using alphanumeric substitution," he said happily. "No shifts. Stupidly simple. The sort of password that longs to be cracked."

Ada had, long ago, memorized a table that listed each letter next to its corresponding number, 1 through 26. She turned the dials on the combination lock—3 for *C*, 15 for *O*—until they read *31545*, and then pressed two buttons to its right and left, and the latches opened with a satisfying, muted pop.

Inside, the briefcase was empty, lined with a silk material that was yellowing in places. One half of the briefcase bore little elasticized compartments meant to hold writing implements and notepads, and David now took a pen from his shirt pocket and tucked it into place inside one. He walked back into his office and came out again holding an unlined pad of white paper, stationery from the Steiner Lab that David had ordered en masse five years ago. He handed this to Ada as well.

"There," he said. "Now you're all ready."

"Shall I walk you to school?" he asked her.

"I'll be okay," said Ada. In fact she would have liked him to, but she wanted to demonstrate to him that she'd be all right—to show him that she was grown up now, to lessen his guilt, which, that month, had manifested itself in ways that Ada had begun to notice. He looked at her for longer than usual; he asked her more often what she'd like to do in the evening or on weekends. A dark shadow crossed his brow now whenever he could not locate a word or phrase, which happened many times each day. The night before, in the middle of a glass of sherry, he had apologized to her.

"I should not have put you in the position in which you now find yourself," said David. "I was trying to do what I thought was right, but I fear I've made everything worse."

"I'll be all right," Ada had said, reassuringly.

"Oh, my dear. I feel as if I'm throwing you to the wolves," said David. "Genuflecting to the cross. Learning the rosary. Confessing your sins to Father So-and-So. Good heavens," he said.

He took a pensive sip.

"Sometimes I still think I should have sent you to public school," he said. "But Liston knows best, I suppose."

He had packed both of them lunches the night before, as he often did, but that day, for the first time, Ada would be taking hers separately. Carrying it herself. She put the brown bag inside her briefcase, squashing it slightly when she closed it, feeling the give of the bread. They walked together over the bridge and then, at the main intersection that followed, Ada turned left and David turned right.

"What is it that I tell you here?" asked David. "Have a good day, I suppose?"

His face looked pinched, slightly red around the nose. Ada stood apart from him: she did not know how to comfort him. She needed comforting herself.

He looked at her ruefully. "Don't take them too seriously," he said finally. "Don't take anything too much to heart, Ada. All right?"

She nodded solemnly. And then she watched her father as he walked away, carrying his own briefcase down by his side. She longed in that moment to go with him: to run after him, to sigh deeply and contentedly as she settled into her work at the lab. Instead she turned, finally, and walked in the opposite direction. Her head was down, like David's head. From above, they would have looked like mirror images of one another, one larger, one smaller: a Rorschach test; a paper snowflake, unfolded; two noblemen pacing away from one another in preparation for a duel.

It was a short walk to Queen of Angels from there. She tightened her right hand around the handle of the briefcase; it made her feel professional, secure, as if she were clasping her father's hand. When she arrived, she found she was alone. No other students were in sight; and the first-floor windows were too high to see inside from street level. Ada walked up the steps, feeling increasingly ill at ease. At the top of them, she tried the handle of a door and found that it was locked. She tried another. Locked. She stood for a moment outside, wondering about her next move; a large part of her wanted to turn and walk home. *I tried,* she imagined saying. *The door was locked.* She did not feel yet that she had any obligation to the school; she did not feel, yet, that she lacked agency, or the right of self-governance. In her life, Ada had rarely been told that she could not do something she wished to do, because all of her desires aligned so completely with the desires of those around her, because her deference to her father and all of his colleagues meant that her requests were usually very reasonable and very small. All of her life she had operated in the world of adults, and the world of adults had welcomed her.

Now she decided that it was reasonable that she turn and walk home, but as she reached the bottom of the steps, one of the dark blue doors opened behind her and a low voice issued forth.

"Where do you think you're going?" said the voice.

Ada turned around. The man in the doorway was small and stern. He had gray hair parted sharply to the side of his head, and brown pants, and a wide, short, brown tie.

"Nowhere," she said. She was surprised into saying it.

"Were you leaving?" the man asked.

"I was trying to get in," said Ada. "The door was locked."

"And knocking is something you're not familiar with?" he asked her. She had never been spoken to in this way, so harshly.

"I'm new," said Ada, by way of explanation. She began to dig in the pockets of her skirt for her schedule so she could show him, but the man was already coming toward her. Shockingly, he took her by her elbow. She had not ever been handled in this way. He brought her forward, up the steps, pushing her ahead of him as if she might try to escape. And once she was inside he pulled the door closed behind her with a crack.

It was explained to her by the secretary, when she reached the office, that although her first class began at 8:00 a.m., homeroom was at 7:40 sharp. The front doors were closed and locked at 7:38 a.m. exactly, and after that students were required to ring a bell to be let in, and their lateness was noted on their record. Ada was certain that this had not been explained to her on her first and only visit to the school, but it felt futile to protest—they were so certain of her guilt that it seemed better, more effective, to hang her head and nod.

The secretary, Mrs. Duggan, donned her half-moon reading glasses to take a look at the schedule that she still held in both of her hands. She glanced up at the clock on the wall.

"8:01," she said. "You should be in Sister Margaret's class right now." And she walked Ada out of the office, down a short hallway, around a corner.

"If you'd gone to your homeroom you would have gotten your locker assignment. But we should get you to class now. You'll get it tomorrow," said Mrs. Duggan.

Although it hadn't occurred to her yesterday, Ada now noticed the smell of the place—the famous schoolhouse smell she had read about in many of her favorite books. Chalk and soap and dust and metal. She took it in. Overhead, fluorescent lights flickered from time to time distractingly.

She reached Sister Margaret's classroom, and Mrs. Duggan turned to her.

"I'll introduce you to your student ambassador first," she said. "You were supposed to meet her this morning."